THE
INJUDICIOUS
JUDGE

Michael Underwood

THE INJUDICIOUS JUDGE

ST. MARTIN'S PRESS
NEW YORK

Library of Congress Cataloging-in-Publication Data

Underwood, Michael, 1916-
    The injudicious judge / by Michael Underwood.
        p.   cm.
        ISBN 0-312-01447-3 : $15.95
        I. Title.
    PR6055.V315   1988   87-29934
    823'.914—dc19   CIP

First published in Great Britain by Macmillan London Limited.

First U.S. Edition

10 9 8 7 6 5 4 3 2 1

THE
INJUDICIOUS
JUDGE

CHAPTER 1

'We'll get you for this, you spiteful old cow!'

The court's accoustics were excellent and every word could be clearly heard. There was a slight scuffle as the police officer responsible for order in the public gallery closed in on the man who had created the disturbance and tried to drag him from his seat. Almost immediately the woman next to him started to scream obscenities at the judge.

It was several minutes before order was restored, during which time the one person who remained wholly composed was Her Honour Judge Celia Kilby. She just sat quietly waiting for the next defendant to appear in the dock to be sentenced. It was a day on which she was dealing with a succession of pleas of guilty, which she did expeditiously and with as much emotion as a mediaeval executioner.

She was always tough on burglars and it was her sentence of six years on one named Patrick Pashley that had provoked the outburst in the public gallery from his wife, Shirley, and brother, Dan.

Patrick Pashley himself was so stunned by the severity of his sentence (he'd been expecting a maximum of four years) that he was back in a cell beneath the court-room before it had sunk in. By then all he could do was shout and bang on the wall with his fists. But just as the court's accoustics were near perfect, so its cells were virtually sound-proof. Thus Judge Kilby was able to proceed undisturbed and it wasn't long before the next defendant was on his way to prison.

Peter Duxbury turned and gave Rosa Epton, his instructing solicitor, a dubious smile.

'She certainly got out of bed the wrong side this morning,' he murmured.

'She does every morning,' Rosa remarked.

She was still cross that the counsel she had originally briefed was not going to appear. It had been an all too familiar story. At five o'clock the previous evening the clerk of the Chambers had phoned to say that unfortunately the counsel she had instructed was still part heard in the Court of Appeal, where the

1

case in which he was appearing had not finished as expected.

'But not to worry, Miss Epton,' the clerk had gone on breezily with all the confidence of a super salesman, 'I've had young Mr Duxbury read the papers and I know you'll not be disappointed in him. He's one of the bright young stars in our Chambers and he'll not let you down.'

On meeting Peter Duxbury at court that morning, Rosa's first impression had not been entirely favourable. He might be a bright young star, but it had struck her that he'd already acquired some of his profession's less attractive characteristics. A tendency towards complacence and an indulgent use of legal jargon were two such, neither being appropriate to a plea in mitigation on behalf of someone charged with stealing ladies' underwear on a grand scale.

She hoped, however, that her initial reservation might prove ill-founded. He had certainly read his brief and seemed full of self-confidence, but then he had never yet appeared before Judge Kilby.

'Usher, will you kindly stop moving about. It's most distracting.'

The judge's quiet but authoritative tone caused everyone to freeze in their places. The hapless court usher, a homely, middle-aged woman, quickly sat down and stared demurely at the floor with hands folded in her lap. Palpable waves of sympathy flowed in her direction.

Cedric Duthie, who was Rosa's client, came into the dock and she turned to give him a quick smile of encouragement. She had warned him that, in view of his previous record, he was bound to go to prison. The only question being for how long. It was not an easy case in which to mitigate, hence Rosa's annoyance at not having the counsel of her choice to make the plea.

In answer to the clerk, Duthie admitted the charges put to him with a cheerfulness that ill became his situation.

'Between you and me, Miss Epton,' he had earlier confided in Rosa, 'courts bring out the best in me. I respond to the occasion. I enjoy being the centre of attention. With the judge and the barristers all dressed up in their wigs and robes, I really feel I'm somebody.'

2

As he pleaded to the indictment, Judge Kilby observed him as a spider might contemplate a fly caught in its web.

Prosecuting counsel outlined the facts of the case in dispassionate language, referring to the items of female underwear that the defendant had stolen with no more emotion than if they'd been so many brown paper bags. He told the court that the defendant also wanted a number of other offences to be taken into consideration when he was sentenced, adding, 'Not all relating to female nether garments, Your Honour.'

A police officer then went into the witness box and gave Duthie's antecedent history to the court. He was forty-seven years old, he said, and had no fixed employment.

'He'd hardly have had time to follow any regular employment with his record,' the judge observed acidly.

'I agree, Your Honour,' the officer said with a sycophantic grin.

'Do you wish to ask the officer any questions, Mr Duxbury?' Judge Kilby enquired.

'Tell me, Officer, has Mr Duthie . . .'

'Mr Duxbury,' the judge intervened sharply, 'in this court he's not Mister anybody, he's the defendant.'

'If Your Honour pleases,' counsel said in a tone that implied his concern with more important things. Turning back to the witness he went on, 'Has the defendant shown you every co-operation throughout your enquiry?'

'Yes.'

'The officer may know what you mean,' the judge broke in, 'but I don't.'

Rosa observed her counsel turn a shade of pink as he faltered before replying.

'I mean, Your Honour, has the defendant been helpful to the officer?'

'As opposed to obstructing him and aggravating the offences to which he has pleaded guilty?' the judge enquired with a contemptuous sniff.

'With the greatest respect, Your Honour, I submit that my question was perfectly clear and reasonable in the circumstances,' Peter Duxbury said hotly, while Rosa squirmed in her seat.

3

Though her sympathies were with counsel, it was her client's fate she was most concerned about. It seemed that the judge had taken an immediate dislike to counsel and was set to give him a rough time. And that meant a poor outlook for the defendant.

The officer in charge of the case, who had no particular love for judges or barristers, having suffered at the hands of both, was content to see others shed blood. In answer to further questions he conceded that the defendant had never shown violence in the course of his criminal career, but refused to speculate on whether he was in need of psychiatric help.

'He never sold for profit any of the underwear he stole, did he?' Duxbury asked.

'No, he kept it in an old trunk in his room.'

'Do you know whether he used to put any of it on sometimes?'

Judge Kilby tapped her notebook with her pen in a gesture that the court regulars recognised as a storm signal.

'Well, answer the question,' Duxbury barked, when the witness hesitated.

'Mr Duxbury,' the judge said in an icy tone, 'the defendant has pleaded guilty to theft and I assure you it won't assist the court to explore any prurient by-ways, such as you propose.'

'I was hoping to satisfy Your Honour that my client really is in need of psychiatric treatment . . .'

'Then you can save your energies, as well as the court's time,' Judge Kilby said tartly.

'With the greatest respect, Your Honour, I'm entitled to ask any relevant questions I wish.'

By this time Peter Duxbury's face had turned a deeper red and his voice became tense. All Rosa felt able to do was sit tight and hope. To try and whisper calming sentiments into his ear was unlikely to achieve any good. What she did do was silently curse the clerk in Peter Duxbury's Chambers for his choice of replacement.

'Your question was irrelevant,' the judge said. 'Now will you kindly get on and not waste the court's time.'

'If I'm prevented from putting the questions I wish, I have

nothing further to ask him,' counsel said and promptly sat down. Turning round to Rosa, he said in a furious whisper, 'She's a bitch and not fit to be a judge.'

'You've still got to make a plea in mitigation,' Rosa said helplessly. 'I suggest you keep it short.'

'The court's waiting, Mr Duxbury,' Judge Kilby broke in. 'Perhaps you would do it the courtesy of not keeping everyone in suspense while you whisper to your instructing solicitor.'

Peter Duxbury rose to his feet and took a deep breath. Rosa could see that he was shaking with emotion. If he couldn't cope with judicial bullying, he wouldn't survive for long in a highly competitive profession. After all, Judge Kilby was by no means the only member of the Bench to throw her judicial weight around.

'I ask Your Honour to put aside all preconceived notions about my client,' he began, but got no further.

'I will put that remark down to your inexperience and ignore its impertinence,' the judge said coldly. 'This court does not have preconceived notions about any of the defendants who appear before it.'

Rosa thought for a desperate moment that counsel was about to pick up his papers and stalk out of court. There seemed to be an endless silence while Peter Duxbury wrestled with his emotions and the judge continued to stare at him.

At last he spoke. 'If Your Honour doesn't wish to hear me further, it would be better to say so and I'll take the matter to the Court of Appeal.'

'Aren't you being both premature and somewhat presumptuous, Mr Duxbury? As far as I'm aware you don't have any grounds of appeal. The defendant has pleaded guilty to these distasteful offences and consequently the only appeal will lie against sentence and that stage has not yet been reached. Am I right?'

'Yes,' counsel said in a strangulated voice.

'Very well, I'm still waiting to hear your plea in mitigation, so shall we get on?'

Somehow counsel managed to string together a dozen sentences which passed for a not very effective plea in mitigation. He did, however, suggest that the offences indicated a morbid streak in the defendant's nature which psychiatric treatment might help to eradicate.

When he sat down, Rosa could see rivulets of sweat pouring down the back of his neck. Even his wig looked as if it had been caught in the rain. She turned to glance at Cedric Duthie, who was wearing, as well he might, a slightly bemused expression. He immediately flashed her a cheerful smile. A moment later the clerk of the court asked him whether he had anything to say before sentence was passed.

He stood up and beamed at the judge who quickly looked away.

'I should just like to thank everyone,' he said in an ingratiating voice. 'The police, my counsel and Miss Epton, as well as Your Honour who, I know, will treat me fairly. We all have our funny little ways and mine have led me here. Mind you, I've not always had that particular urge and I can't tell you why I do it. Maybe a psychiatrist could help me, if Your Honour thought it a good idea. Anyway, that's all I want to say . . . Oh, yes, there was one other thing. It's the first time I've appeared in front of a lady judge. It's always nice to have a first in one's life and I'm grateful to Your Honour for being the one to provide such a memorable occasion.'

Everyone glanced towards Judge Kilby who appeared as surprised as the rest of her court. But she quickly pulled herself together.

'Cedric Duthie,' she said, 'I regard you as a social pest rather than a hardened criminal. Whether or not you could benefit from psychiatric treatment, I don't pretend to know. For the offences to which you have pleaded guilty and for those you have asked to have taken into consideration, I sentence you to eighteen months' imprisonment.'

A moment later the court had adjourned and Judge Kilby and the defendant had made their separate exits, leaving Rosa and Peter Duxbury standing in an awkward silence.

The fact that Cedric Duthie had received a lighter sentence than expected was, perversely, due to counsel's unfortunate passage at arms with the judge. Judge Kilby was obviously aware that she had over-stepped the mark and had therefore decided to pass a sentence against which an appeal couldn't be justified. Rosa had known it happen before when trial judges didn't wish their conduct to be scrutinised by their senior brethren.

What had happened in court had been to Duthie's advantage, so that all was well that ended well. Rosa was reflecting sardonically on this when Peter Duxbury spoke.

'I'll not let her get away with it,' he said savagely. 'I won't have her wreck my career.' Through clenched teeth he added, 'I could kill her with my own hands.'

Rosa felt embarrassed by such melodramatic threats, particularly as they were obviously overheard by a number of people on their way out of court, including a press reporter whose nose gave an immediate eager twitch.

Normally she would have gone to the cells to have a few comforting words with her client, but it struck her that, on this occasion, counsel was in greater need of solace than the ever chirpy Cedric Duthie.

'I'll meet you outside,' she said to Peter Duxbury, 'and we'll go and have a drink.'

On her way out of court, an elderly barrister politely held a door open for her.

'Just another typical day in the life of our beloved Judge Kilby,' he remarked with a dry cackle as Rosa passed him.

It was, in fact, Thursday, 22nd May. A day on which events yet to come cast their first ominous shadow.

CHAPTER 2

Rosa let out a sigh of relief when Peter Duxbury eventually departed to return to his Chambers. Two large gin and tonics had done nothing to alleviate his mood of smouldering resentment. His general air of self-satisfaction had been seriously dented, revealing a vulnerability to which he didn't wish to admit.

'The sooner you get back into court, the better,' Rosa had

said, as he continued to gaze morosely into his glass. 'It's like driving again immediately after you've been involved in an accident.'

'She's a monster,' he said in a brooding tone. 'She should be removed from the Bench.'

'I agree she gave you a rough ride . . .'

'Rough ride! She deliberately set out to humiliate me. Word'll go around and my practice is bound to suffer.' He gave Rosa a bitter look. 'Would you ever brief me again after today?'

'You're being melodramatic,' Rosa said, uncomfortably aware that the truthful answer was 'no'. But then she hadn't briefed him in the first place. He had stood in for Charles Provis. She glanced at her watch. 'I think I'll go back to court and have a word with our client before he's carted off to prison. He, at least, is a happy man; he was expecting something much worse.'

Peter Duxbury smiled sourly. 'If they want to do him a real favour, they should put him in a women's prison.'

'I doubt whether he'd find their underwear would hold the same appeal.'

They had been drinking in a pub about a quarter of a mile from the court and, after dropping Duxbury off at the nearest underground station, Rosa returned there. The afternoon session had begun, but she had no urge to find out whether Judge Kilby had mellowed with lunch. It seemed improbable.

'Hello, Miss Epton, what a nice surprise,' Duthie said when they met in the cell area beneath the court-room. 'I've just been given an excellent lunch. I hope you've had something to eat, too.'

Rosa smiled. Surely even Cedric Duthie must have his black moments, though not apparently on a day out in court. It was as though he'd been given a treat.

'I'm glad your sentence wasn't as heavy as it might have been,' she said.

'I thought the judge turned out to be a very nice lady. So chic, too. Not at all an old battle-axe.'

Well, at least Judge Kilby had one fan, Rosa reflected.

'I expect you'll go to Wormwood Scrubs,' she said. 'At any

8

rate for the first part of your sentence.'

'Don't worry about me, Miss Epton. I'm a survivor. I'll be all right.'

'Good. The important thing will be to stay out of trouble after your release.'

'Sufficient unto the day is the evil thereof. Isn't that what the Bible says? I'm not a religious man myself, but I always sign on for church when I'm inside.'

Rosa got up and they shook hands. As she made her way out of the building, she reflected that Peter Duxbury could have learnt quite a few lessons about life from their client. It took her thirty minutes to drive back to her office in West London where a pile of paperwork awaited her.

It was towards the end of the working day that Stephanie, their office telephonist-cum-receptionist-cum-vital force, announced that the clerk of Mr Duxbury's Chambers would like to have a word with her.

'Miss Epton, this is Martin. What on earth went wrong at court this morning? Mr Duxbury has returned to Chambers in what I can only call a profound state of shock. I've never seen him so upset. What happened?'

'I'm afraid Judge Kilby took an obvious dislike to him and decided to make things as difficult as she could for him.'

'We all know that she's not the easiest of judges.'

'That could be called an understatement.'

'But what did he do to upset her?'

Rosa sighed. 'If I may say so, Mr Duxbury gives the unfortunate appearance of being rather pleased with himself. This obviously grated on the judge, who determined to deflate him. Quite honestly, what surprised *me* was his inability to cope.'

'Oh dear, oh dear! Perhaps he's gone too far too fast. But I do assure you, Miss Epton, that he's highly thought of in Chambers and has handled some quite difficult cases since he's been with us.'

'Perhaps it was his first experience of an awkward judge. Pride comes before a fall, to use a tired old proverb.'

When the clerk spoke again it was in a slow, thoughtful tone.

9

'I wonder if what happened can be explained on psychological grounds.'

'Meaning?'

'He was recently jilted by the girl he was engaged to. He took it badly and we all felt very sorry for him at the time. It happened a few months ago. It could be that appearing before a female judge caused him to over-compensate.'

'Could be.' Rosa said, doubtfully.

He had been more than jilted by Judge Kilby. She had knocked him to the ground and then trampled on him. It could be enough to put him off women for the rest of his life.

'Well, I'm terribly sorry things went so wrong, Miss Epton,' the clerk now went on. 'Especially as Mr Duxbury was standing in for Mr Provis. I hope you won't hold it against these Chambers.'

'In the event, as you've probably heard, the client got away rather lightly.'

'Was that because the judge realised she'd gone too far and didn't want to be taken to the Court of Appeal?'

'That would be my guess.'

'We'll have to do what we can to restore Mr Duxbury's confidence.' He paused and went on in a silky tone. 'If you could see your way to sending him a brief, Miss Epton, I'm sure that would go a long way to helping his morale.'

'If something suitable comes up, I'll bear him in mind.' Rosa said.

It was one of those pious statements that cost nothing and seem harmless enough at the time.

CHAPTER 3

Judge Kilby completed her afternoon's work shortly before four o'clock and retired to her room.

She was well aware that she was not a popular judge, but the knowledge didn't bother her. In her view, if a judge was to perform properly, there was no room for sentiment or what she regarded as cheap popularity. She was not given to witty comments or cosy homilies. If the result was to give her court the attraction of a Siberian labour camp in winter. she didn't mind.

Nevertheless, she regarded herself as being in tune with public opinion. For example, burglaries were on the increase, therefore those who perpetrated them must expect condign punishment. Pleas in mitigation rarely moved her. Indeed, she sometimes cynically reflected that every criminal had a dying mother or a sickly wife waiting in the wings to soften a judge's heart. Her own remained generally unaffected by the visions that were conjured up by defending counsel.

She took off her judicial robes and hung them up, having first removed her wig and tidied her hair, which she wore short. She had always thought that female barristers looked particularly absurd with hair cascading down beneath their wigs, however beautiful that hair might be. Her own was a fairly undistinguished dark brown, but neat to a fault.

Divested of her judicial trappings, she could have passed for the manageress of an exclusive Mayfair boutique. She was wearing a smartly cut black dress with maroon trimmed neckline and sleeves and at fifty-two her figure was as good as it had been thirty years earlier. Cedric Duthie had been right to call her chic.

A nearby church clock struck four while she was deciding whether to leave immediately or stay and write a letter.

For the past fifteen years she had lived in the first-floor flat of a converted house in SW19. It was rented accommodation and she had no intention of moving, despite the machinations of her landlord who wanted to get vacant possession of the building.

Bernard Riscock had bought 8 Aubusson Way as an investment a few years earlier and had been conducting a running battle with his tenants ever since. He had been misled into believing that he wouldn't have any trouble buying them out, but he had reckoned without Judge Celia Kilby, who not only thwarted him at every turn but frequently took the offensive on behalf of herself and her three fellow residents.

Riscock wasn't used to being frustrated, particularly by a woman (all the tenants were female apart from one elderly widower), and had recently been wondering whether a discreetly hired heavy mob might not now be his last resort. Where persuasion and cajolery had failed, crude intimidation might succeed.

Celia Kilby, who didn't put anything beyond him, had decided to go on the offensive once more. Hence a letter to him saying she hoped he wouldn't be tempted to take any action that could put him outside the law. Let their unscrupulous landlord take heed!

Eight Aubusson Way was a pleasant late Victorian house with a secluded garden. It lay in a quiet, sunny tree-lined road and Celia Kilby's flat on the first floor was the nicest and most spacious. Moreover, she had decorated and furnished it with considerable taste. It was there that her regular bridge four would be meeting for their weekly game that evening, it being her turn to play host. The other members were Adèle Spicer, a wealthy divorcee who lived close by, Norman Ackroyd, an elderly bachelor who had a large house with a live-in staff on Kingston Hill, and Giles Crowhurst who was a barrister in Celia's old Chambers. He lived in a tiny flat not far from the Temple, so was unable to take his turn at offering hospitality.

Bridge was the bond that held them together. They played keenly and seriously. Celia Kilby was probably the best player and Giles Crowhurst the weakest, although there wasn't much to choose between any of them.

Judge Kilby sealed and stamped the letter to her landlord and prepared to leave for the day. She was looking forward to an evening of bridge.

The established routine was for the three visiting players to arrive at the appointed rendezvous at eight o'clock when drinks would be served and pleasantries exchanged. At eight-fifteen they would sit down and start playing. A break would be taken around ten o'clock when coffee and light snacks would be served. Play would then resume and continue until around midnight.

In her usual orderly way, Celia Kilby had everything laid out and ready by seven-thirty. Five minutes later her doorbell rang

12

and she frowned with annoyance. She knew quite well who it was. Giles Crowhurst always arrived early when play was at her flat. She wished he wouldn't. He had never got over the pangs of unrequited love where Celia was concerned. Though he was six years younger he had been hopefully in love with her since they first met. He was one of those amiable, but decidedly ineffectual people. As ineffectual in the pursuit of love as in his career at the Bar, although remaining quietly persistent.

Celia opened her front door to be confronted by her gently smiling guest.

'Sorry if I'm a bit early,' he said, as he always did, before stepping forward and kissing her lightly on a distinctly cool cheek. 'What sort of day have you had?'

'One burglary's very much like another,' she replied with a deprecating smile.

'Is that the only sort of case you've had all day?'

'Very nearly. Seven, all pleas of guilty, and an unpleasant little man who went in for stealing women's underwear. And he was represented by an incompetent young counsel.'

'What was his name?'

'Duxbury.'

'Never heard of him.'

'He doesn't merit being heard of again.' She led the way into her large, comfortably furnished drawing-room. 'How are things in Chambers?'

'Malcolm's just flown out to Hong Kong to appear in some multi-million pound civil action. He only got back from something similar in Bermuda at the weekend. He earns enough to pay off the national debt. Robert's hoping to become a circuit judge . . .'

'Robert Fisherton?'

'Yes.'

'They'll be scraping the barrel if he's appointed.'

'I'm told he's done rather well when he's been sitting in an acting capacity. But the spiciest item of news is that Howard is about to re-marry.' Giles Crowhurst paused before adding with a mischievous smile, 'To a girl of twenty-four. He met her at the Bar golf meeting. She was serving behind the bar at the club

13

where the meeting was held.'

'Howard must be all of sixty.'

'Sixty-two to be exact. She'll be his fourth wife.' He gave Celia a wistful smile. 'And I'm still hoping that one day you'll be my first.'

'Oh, for heaven's sake, Giles,' she said with a touch of exasperation.

'Things could be very different when I've got this job in Brussels. I now realise that I should have quit the Bar earlier. As soon as it was apparent I was never going to make the big time. But once I'm settled in Brussels, I hope you'll see things differently. I'm sure we could reach an agreement whereby we carried on with our respective jobs. We could spend alternate weekends in London and Brussels. Something of that sort. And there'd be all the vacations we could have together.'

Celia Kilby frowned. 'Have you definitely got the EEC job?'

'I've not yet received the offer, but I'm most hopeful. Incidentally, have they got in touch with you for a reference?' She shook her head as though to fend off a mosquito. 'I'm sure they'll be approaching you soon,' he went on. 'They can't fail to be impressed by my having a judge as a referee.'

At that moment, the doorbell rang.

'That'll be Adèle and Norman. He was picking her up on his way.'

'Anything I can do while you're letting them in?'

'No, everything's ready.'

'Then I'll just get myself a glass of water from the kitchen.'

Giles Crowhurst and his glasses of water were another source of irritation to her. Moreover she disliked the way he roamed around her flat as if it were his own. She always made a particular point of firmly closing her bedroom door before he came.

'My dear, are you all right?' Adèle Spicer said as she sailed in.

'Perfectly. Why do you ask?'

'I read in the evening paper how someone shouted threats at you in court. It must have been awful.'

'Good gracious no! You get used to that sort of thing when you're a judge.'

14

Mrs Spicer shuddered. 'Then I'm certainly glad I'm not one.'

She had a large, moonlike face, crowned by a mass of heavily lacquered golden hair and invariably smelt of talcum powder. Her wrists were weighted down with chunks of costume jewellery.

'Giles not here yet?' she sang out as she passed into the drawing-room.

'He's in the kitchen.' Celia said, as she hung up Norman Ackroyd's coat. It was the same coat he had been wearing, winter and summer, all the time she had known him. In winter, however, there was the addition of a scarf. He was a spry eighty year old who made few concessions to changing temperatures.

'It's taken you a long time to fetch a glass of water,' Celia remarked when Giles returned to the room a minute or two later.

'I took the opportunity of washing my hands as well.' he replied, with an unwonted touch of asperity.

Shortly afterwards they sat down for the first rubber. They had, as usual, cut for partners and Celia found herself playing with Norman Ackroyd. It was better that way as being partnered by Giles could lead to acerbic post mortems.

The evening progressed with only desultory conversation between games which was chiefly confined to the lie of the cards. By the time they reached their break, Celia and her partner were well up. Giles Crowhurst seemed to be in a withdrawn mood. He had been holding rotten cards and gave the impression of having lost interest in the outcome.

'Buck up, partner.' Adèle Spicer said heartily, as she popped a small smoked salmon sandwich into her mouth. 'We've got to do better. We can't let them get away with this.'

'That's right,' he said in an abstracted fashion.

'These are delicious, Celia,' Mrs Spicer went on, as she helped herself to another sandwich. 'Where do you buy your smoked salmon? Fortnum and Mason?'

'Usually Marks and Spencer, but this lot came from a place in Sussex.'

'When were you down in Sussex?' Giles asked with a sudden frown.

'Yesterday as a matter of fact. I had a day off from court and drove down. I visited a friend,' she added in a tone that carried a definite taunt.

When play resumed, Giles and his partner continued with their run of bad luck and finished the evening out of pocket. Debts were paid and the guests prepared to leave. Giles normally insisted on helping with the clearing-up after the others had gone, which used to make Celia irritable. She didn't want him hanging around and she always got rid of him as quickly as she could. On this particular evening she had decided that she really would push him out with the others.

In the event, however, he not only didn't offer to stay and clear up, but left ahead of his fellow guests.

'Giles didn't seem himself this evening,' Adèle observed after he had departed. 'I hope he's all right.'

'He's always suffered from bouts of depression,' Celia said.

'Is he likely to become a judge one day?'

'I wouldn't think so,' Celia replied in a studied tone.

'He's such a sweet, kind man.'

'That doesn't mean he'd make a good judge.'

'I suppose not. Well, see you next Thursday at my place, dear.'

The following day, Friday, Judge Kilby began trying a case that was due to last the best part of a week. It involved two young men who were jointly charged with offences of assault, theft and malicious damage. They looked highly pleased with themselves as they sat in the dock listening to prosecuting counsel outlining the case against them. From time to time they would snigger and exchange grins with friends in the public gallery.

Judge Kilby decided that they needed to be reminded of their precarious situation at the earliest possible moment. For some reason, inexplicable to her, the magistrates before whom they had earlier appeared had granted them pre-trial bail and she determined to put an end to that.

Their expressions of stunned surprise, followed by fury, when at the end of the day their bail was revoked, gave her grim satisfaction.

On Saturday morning she drove down to Sussex for the weekend, returning to London late on Sunday night.

It was on Tuesday, 27th May that the letter arrived, addressed to her at court. She was vaguely aware of her name being misspelt on the envelope, Kilby appearing as Kilbey. In any event the hand-writing looked uneducated.

Inside was a single sheet of ruled paper, apparently torn from a cheap notebook. The words on it were printed in black ballpoint and read:

YOU SIGNED YOUR DEATH WARRANT
LAST THURSDAY. AWAIT EXECUTION.

CHAPTER 4

'Come along to my room, Stephen. I wish to have a word with you.'

'Yes, right away.'

Stephen Hicks, the clerk of the court, always reacted promptly to Judge Kilby's demands. Though he addressed her by her first name when they were talking in private, he never felt completely at ease doing so and he wouldn't have dreamt of taking any liberties with her. Whenever he was summoned to her room, he was invariably reminded of the times he was sent for at school by the headmaster. As then, one hoped for the best, but prepared for the worst.

He found her sitting at her desk robed for court apart from her wig which lay on a chair looking like a hairy mollusc.

'Good morning, Celia,' he said in a tentatively cheerful tone.

'Read this,' she said, handing him the anonymous note.

He read it twice with an increasingly grave expression.

'Last Thursday was the day you dealt with all those pleas and ... yes, of course, there was the disturbance in the public gallery when you sentenced that man Pashley. My guess is that one of his family or friends has sent this.'

'Possibly.'

'I don't think you ought to let it worry you too greatly. People

17

who issue these sort of threats never carry them out.' He had nearly used the word 'execute' instead of 'carry out', but saved himself in time from such a tactless slip of the tongue.

'I'm not unduly worried, but obviously the matter must be reported.'

'Yes, of course. Would you like me to phone the local station and get an officer along?'

'Threatening a judge is not a matter for some overworked Detective Sergeant,' she said disdainfully. 'I want you to call the Yard and get them to send an officer of suitable experience. Say that I will see him between one and two o'clock while the court's adjourned.' She glanced at her watch. 'You'd better get on with it straight away, otherwise we shall be late starting.' As he moved towards the door, she added, 'And, Stephen, don't tell anyone – and I mean *anyone* – about the letter.'

'Of course not. I'll make sure nobody overhears my call to the Yard.'

'Good.'

'Perhaps I'd better take the letter with me.'

'I'd sooner keep it. You won't need it anyway.'

Fifteen minutes later when she took her seat on the Bench, Stephen Hicks turned and whispered to her that an officer would be there at one o'clock. She received the information with a brief nod.

When the court adjourned, she retired immediately to her room where her lunch awaited her on a tray. It was always the same. Black coffee and a cottage cheese sandwich made of wholemeal bread.

She hadn't been there long when the clerk called her on the internal phone.

'I have Detective Chief Inspector Chantry with me,' he announced. 'Shall I bring him along?'

'I'll be ready to see him in five minutes,' she said.

She quickly ate her lunch and then placed the tray over on a side table. Apart from removing her wig she kept her robes on during the midday adjournment, and she now combed her hair and applied some lipstick. A quick glance at herself in the mirror and she was ready.

18

Her feelings towards the police were almost clinically neutral. They received no preferential treatment in her court, but equally she didn't encourage copper-bashing by defending counsel. The police for their part regarded her with some favour. Any judge who dished out tough sentences was apt to meet with their approval.

Detective Chief Inspector Alan Chantry of CI, New Scotland Yard, was in his late thirties and had been a policeman for nearly twenty years. During that time he had held a variety of jobs ranging from being a PC on the beat to serving as a detective inspector on the District Regional Crime Squad. His promotion had been fairly rapid and nobody imagined that he was yet near the peak of his career. He belonged to the relatively new breed of police officer at home in any company. He was an articulate and well-read man with a passion for opera when he had the opportunity to indulge it. He dressed neatly and wore his hair neither short nor untidily long. Spectacles gave him a generally studious appearance. He was unmarried and shared a house with an older widowed sister, an arrangement which suited both of them.

He knew Judge Kilby by name and reputation, but had never met her until he stepped into her room.

'I'm Detective Chief Inspector Chantry, madam,' he said as he walked over and shook hands with her. 'I understand you've received a threatening letter. May I see it please?'

Celia Kilby, who was not used to having anyone display such firm initiative in her presence, removed it from beneath a book on her desk and held it out.

'How many people have touched it apart from yourself? I'm thinking of fingerprints.'

'Only Mr Hicks and myself.'

'Perhaps you would remove it from its envelope and lay it open for me to read. That way it won't have my fingerprints as well.'

Without a word Judge Kilby did as she was bidden and the officer lent over her desk to read it. Then he glanced at the envelope.

'Posted in SE7,' he observed. 'That's Charlton or Woolwich,

if I'm not mistaken. Though it's doubtful whether the writer posted it in his own area.'

'In this case, you may find that he does. On the Thursday in question I had abuse shouted at me from the public gallery after I'd sentenced a man named Patrick Pashley. I've checked the record this morning and I see that Pashley lived in SE7. I would also draw your attention to the fact that my name is misspelt.'

'I'd noticed that. Tell me, what form did the abuse take?'

'I was called a spiteful old cow and whoever created the disturbance said they'd get me for it.'

'Can I have the exact words as you recall them?'

Judge Kilby grimaced. 'We'll get you for this, you spiteful old cow.'

'Nothing very original,' Chantry observed a trifle ambiguously. 'Are you due back in court this afternoon?'

'Yes, at two o'clock.'

'What time will you finish?'

'Around four forty-five.'

'I'll come back and see you then, madam. I'll want to know everything that happened that day which might throw light on this letter. Meanwhile, I'll arrange police protection for you. We can't take any chances.'

'I'm not disposed to take this threat too seriously.'

'Maybe not, madam. But you rightly reported it and now it's my responsibility to ensure no harm comes to you.' He slid the letter and envelope into a plastic folder which he took from his briefcase. 'The fact that an oral threat has been followed up by a written one can't be ignored. Anyway, I'm sure you won't be inconvenienced by the steps we take. We'll be as unobtrusive as possible.' He glanced at his watch. 'I'll get things moving, madam, and I'll see you again at five o'clock.'

'I ought to mention, Chief Inspector, that only the clerk and myself know about the letter. I instructed him not to tell anyone.'

'I'm afraid these things have a habit of getting out. Some of your court staff are probably already speculating who I am and what I'm doing here. Your lady usher, for example, was obviously curious when I passed her in the corridor outside.'

20

It was at that moment that there came a knock on the door.

'Yes, who is it?' Judge Kilby called out crossly.

'It's the usher, Your Honour. Counsel would like to speak to you in private before you return to court.'

The judge bit her lip in annoyance. She realised that almost anything she said or did would now only fuel further speculation.

'Tell them I'll be free in ten minutes,' she called back. Turning to Chief Inspector Chantry, she said grimly, 'I take it you can find your own way out.'

By the time the chief inspector returned to Judge Kilby's room shortly after five o'clock, he had achieved all he had set out to do and a bit more.

He had spoken to the Deputy Assistant Commissioner under whose aegis he worked and given him an interim report. He had then made arrangements for the judge's protection and had finally spoken to one of his own trusted aides, Detective Sergeant William Kirkbride, instructing him to dig out everything he could about the Pashley family.

With that accomplished, he had gone across the road to a café for a cup of tea and a sandwich. He was used to irregular meals at irregular hours. He had just sat down with his food when another man entered the otherwise deserted café.

'Detective Chief Inspector Chantry, isn't it?' he said, sitting down at the same table. 'You don't remember me?'

After a second's pause, Chantry said, 'You work on a newspaper and your name's . . . Adrian Flammer.'

'Not bad. We met on the Grayson murder enquiry.'

'I remember.'

'I like to think I was able to help the police on that one. It was largely due to me you got on to the missing chauffeur as quickly as you did.'

'I don't know that my memory's that good,' Chantry observed drily.

'Anyway, I happened to see you arrive at the court this morning and when I learnt that you'd spent the lunch adjournment closeted with Her Honour, I realised something

21

was up. There's a rumour going round that she's received anonymous threats. Correct?'

'I've not heard the rumour,' Chantry replied blandly.

'But has she?'

'No comment.'

'Which means that she has. Do they relate to what happened in court last Thursday?'

'What did happen in court last Thursday?'

'You obviously know about the abuse from the public gallery, but that wasn't all.'

'Go on, tell me what else happened?'

'So you are interested?' Flammer said with a smug grin.

'As you've obviously followed me here, let's hear what you have to say.'

'I wonder if Judge Kilby has told you about the young barrister to whom she gave a roasting. He was defending a weirdo who'd gone about nicking ladies' underwear and she really flayed him.'

'Why?'

'I presume she decided to be a bit bloodier than usual. I've never seen a counsel so visibly angry and upset in court. It was almost embarrassing. Afterwards, I heard him say he'd gladly kill her with his own hands and that he wouldn't let her get away with what she'd done to him.'

'What was his name?'

'Peter Duxbury.'

'And to whom did he say this?'

'He was talking to his instructing solicitor and I happened to overhear what he said on my way out of court.'

'Who was the solicitor?'

'Rosa Epton of Snaith and Epton.'

'Ah!'

'Do you know her, then?'

'We've met.'

Alan Chantry had formed a good impression of Rosa when they had met on a case a few months earlier. He thought she was both attractive and able, and, most important from a police officer's point of view, trustworthy.

22

'So you see, quite a lot happened in the Kilby woman's court last Thursday,' Flammer said with a small nod of triumph. 'What's more that's probably only the tip of the iceberg.'

'What's that supposed to mean?'

'She's a lady with a past.'

'What sort of a past? And how do you know?'

Flammer leaned forward and assumed a conspiratorial pose. 'I've spent a fair amount of time in her court recently and I've become intrigued by her persona. She's so obviously anti-male for a start. She's much softer on female defendants. Did you know that?'

'I understood she was particularly tough on burglars and as that's almost entirely a masculine crime I suppose her attitude could be misinterpreted as anti-male.'

'There's more to it than that. She definitely has a past.'

'And if she has, what's your interest?'

'I told you, I'm intrigued. I want to know what makes her tick.'

'With a view to writing a front page exposé?'

'That'll depend, won't it?'

'Not if you don't wish to be sued for libel, or have to start life afresh in the Solomon Islands.'

Flammer stared pensively at the tip of his cigarette for a moment.

'Perhaps we ought to keep in touch with one another,' he said, meeting Chantry's gaze.

'You know where to reach me if you ever have any information which'll help solve a crime,' Chantry said drily. 'Meanwhile, I'd better get back.'

'Back? To court, do you mean?'

'Yes, to court,' Chantry said with a resigned sigh. 'You're just like a lot of sparrows searching endlessly for crumbs.'

'It's a pity we don't get more credit for the help we give the police.'

'There's a basic clash of interest. To you, crime is only news if it sells more papers. I'm paid by society to catch criminals regardless of their newsworthiness.'

'There are worse causes than selling newspapers.'

'Tell that to the victims of some of your campaigns!'

By the time DCI Chantry returned to the court, Judge Kilby had risen and was waiting for him in her room. She had disrobed and was standing by the window when he entered. He was struck by the trimness of her appearance. She was wearing a steel-grey skirt with a deep-purple silk blouse that had a tunic collar.

'I hope this won't take long, Chief Inspector,' she said before he had time to speak.

'I've brought a tape recorder, so that the interview can be transcribed later.'

'I think I've already told you all I can. The clerk will give you a list of the cases I dealt with last Thursday, for what that's worth.'

'I already have it.'

'Oh!' Fixing him with a dispassionate eye, she went on, 'The more I've thought about it, the less inclined I am to take the threat seriously.'

'But somebody sent you that note.'

'Almost certainly someone connected with the man Pashley.'

Returning her gaze, Chantry said, 'I understood you had something of a barney, if I may use that expression, with counsel in one of the cases. Is that so?'

'Who told you that?' she asked sharply and, when he didn't reply, went on, 'Whoever it was was talking out of turn. Counsel wouldn't stoop to sending judges childish notes.'

Alan Chantry refrained from comment. He certainly wasn't prepared to exclude the legal profession from acts of childishness.

'Nevertheless, perhaps you'd tell me what happened,' he said. 'I understand the barrister's name was Duxbury.'

He watched as Judge Kilby wrestled with her emotions.

'It's quite irrelevant,' she said at length, 'but, if you must know, I did have occasion to reprove the person you mention for his handling of a case. He was a self-assured but incompetent young man, who has a great deal to learn.'

24

'Do you think you may have upset him more than you intended?'

'It was not my intention to upset him, but to control proceedings in my court,' the judge said coldly. 'Anyway, as I've already said, I'm sure you can rule him out of your enquiry. Whatever his shortcomings, he wouldn't do anything so puerile as to write an anonymous note to a judge.'

'Had you ever come across him before?'

'Never.'

'So you don't know anything about him?'

'No, but I still maintain what I've said. Members of the Bar just don't do that sort of thing.'

Chief Inspector Chantry decided not to question this confident assertion.

'Is there anyone else who may have been upset by something you did last Thursday?' he asked with a quizzically raised eyebrow.

A surprising gleam came into Judge Kilby's eye. 'I remember now, it was the day I wrote to my landlord. I'd better explain . . .'

When she'd finished, Chantry said, 'You believe he'd be capable of actually sending you such a note?'

'Yes, I do. He's an extremely unattractive person: moreover, he's obsessed with the idea of getting his tenants out. As long as I'm there, he doesn't have a hope. I'm more than a match for his wiles.'

'Do you think he's a more likely suspect than one of Pashley's relatives?'

'Frankly, no.'

'Your landlord lives in Croydon and the letter was posted in SE7, which presupposes knowledge on his part of what happened in court that day.'

'I'm told there was a report of the outburst in the evening paper. He might have learnt about it that way.'

'I'll check, of course, but it's doubtful whether any news item would have given such detail as Pashley's address.'

'In my experience newspapers rejoice in regaling their

readers with every conceivable personal detail of those who fill their columns,' Judge Kilby remarked scornfully. 'Anyway, that's as far as I can help you. I take it that you'll keep in touch with developments.'

'Of course. I've arranged various protective measures and we'll review the situation in a few days' time.'

'I hope I'm not going to be tailed everywhere I go.'

'I'd like you to let us know in advance when you're going out and where. Do you have many social engagements this week?'

'Bridge at a friend's flat on Thursday evening.'

'We'll make sure you get there and back safely.'

CHAPTER 5

'Miss Epton? This is Detective Chief Inspector Alan Chantry. We met a few months ago on that case involving the son of an MP.'

'If he's in further trouble, I don't want to know,' Rosa broke in with a quick laugh.

'He gave us both a few headaches, didn't he? No, this is something quite different. I'd appreciate it if I might come and have an off-the-record word with you about a certain matter. Would this afternoon be possible?'

'Off the record, did you say?'

'Strictly so.'

'What about?'

'I'd sooner wait and tell you when we meet.'

'As long as you're not going to make difficulties for me *vis à vis* a client . . .'

'I promise I won't do that.'

'All right. What about four o'clock?'

'That'll suit me fine. I'll see you then.'

Talking to a police officer off the record in her own office was not something to which she lightly agreed, but she remembered Chief Inspector Chantry as someone whose integrity she had learnt to respect during their common involvement in the case he had mentioned. Each had helped the other in a somewhat sensitive and squalid affair. She wondered what he wished to see her about and was still wondering when Ben, their lively and resourceful office boy, brought her a cup of coffee to go with her desk lunch.

'I see that judge of yours has been getting threats, telling her she's for the chop,' he said cheerfully, as he put down the cup.

'What on earth are you talking about, Ben?'

'Judge Kilby. It's in my paper. Says she received an anonymous letter threatening to do her in and the police are investigating.'

'I didn't see that in my paper.'

'You miss a lot of juicy items in your sort of paper.'

'Not to mention pictures of bosomy girls.'

'They're for adolescents or guys with the seven year itch,' Ben said scornfully.

Rosa laughed. 'Thanks, anyway, for the information. Tell Stephanie I'm expecting Detective Chief Inspector Chantry at four o'clock.'

'Will do, Miss Epton. Expect she knows already.'

'Tell her all the same.'

So that must be what Chief Inspector Chantry wanted to see her about, although she couldn't think that Cedric Duthie was the author of the threats. He'd be more likely to send her a Valentine card. Suddenly she remembered Peter Duxbury's incautious remarks and the reporter who had passed by at that moment.

It was on the dot of four that Stephanie announced the officer's arrival.

'I appreciate your seeing me at short notice, Miss Epton,' he said as they shook hands. 'Also your not pressing me to be more explicit on the phone.'

'I think I've guessed why you're here, but I'll leave you to tell me.'

'I understand you had a case in Judge Kilby's court last Thursday?' Rosa nodded and he went on, 'Were you there when abuse was shouted at the judge from the public gallery?'

'Yes. She didn't bat an eyelid.'

'She's a tough lady.'

27

'There are other words for her.'

'You don't like her?'

'Let's say, I'm sure I wouldn't like her if I knew her socially, which I don't.'

'Are you aware that she has since received an anonymous death threat?'

'I wasn't when you phoned, but one of our clerks read it in the paper.'

'The fact that it's reached the press hasn't pleased the lady at all. She probably thinks I leaked it, but I didn't. I warned her, however, that it wouldn't remain a secret for long. Meanwhile, I'm in the process of checking on all the people she managed to upset on the day in question.' He opened his briefcase and took out a photocopy of the letter and envelope and passed it across to Rosa. 'I believe the counsel in your case was one of the people who fell foul of her and actually uttered threats against her life.'

Although Rosa had correctly guessed the reason for the visit and had had time to think what she was going to say, she found herself very much on the horns of a dilemma now that the moment of truth had arrived. She wished she could have canvassed the views of her partner, Robin Snaith, but he had been in court all day and she'd had no chance of speaking to him.

'Anything we say to each other is strictly off the record?' she said, as if playing for time.

'Entirely so.'

'It's true my counsel didn't perform very well. Admittedly he was substituting for the person I'd actually briefed, but the judge took against him and proceeded to tear him in shreds. He could do nothing right in her sight and she publicly humiliated him.'

'How'd he take it?'

'Afterwards, still in the heat of the moment, he made some rather intemperate remarks. He felt she had jeopardised his career and said he wouldn't let her get away with it.'

'Did he make any threats of violence?'

'Not serious ones.'

28

'Might he have said that he'd like to kill her with his own hands?'

'Some such rubbish as that. But nothing which could be taken seriously.'

'Do you think he might have written that anonymous note?'

Rosa stared down at the photocopy lying on her desk.

'The trouble about the law is that it makes one both cautious and suspicious,' she said with a wry smile. 'I suppose the truthful answer to your question is that I don't know Peter Duxbury well enough to voice an opinion. What I will say is that, if it was he, I'm sure he'd have no intention of carrying out such threats.'

'The letter was posted on Monday, four days after the events of last Thursday, so it was hardly sent in the heat of the moment.'

'I can't believe he'd have been so incredibly stupid,' Rosa said, though without one hundred per cent conviction.

'It's worse than stupid. Sending a letter threatening to murder is a criminal offence, as you know.'

'Another reason why I can't believe it was Peter Duxbury. He'd hardly put himself in that sort of jeopardy.'

'Are you saying that because he's a lawyer?'

'Because he has too much to lose.'

'But if he thought his career had already been ruined . . .'

'That's nonsense.'

'I thought professional reputations could be made or broken by a single incident.'

'Not by a mere plea in mitigation before a circuit judge,' Rosa said firmly. 'I'll tell you something else I'm sure of, namely that Judge Kilby will be with us for a long time to come.'

'I hope so. For my own sake if nobody else's,' Chantry remarked drily. 'It certainly wouldn't help *my* career if the threats became a reality.'

'Are you proposing to interview Peter Duxbury?'

'I'll be interviewing everyone who could have had a motive. I've already seen Pashley's wife and his brother.'

'Any admissions?'

He shook his head. 'Only vigorous denials. Needless to say, I'm obtaining specimens of everyone's handwriting in the hope that the lab will be able to come up with something. I dictate the exact words that appeared and hope somebody will give something away. So far Pashley's wife spelt Kilby with two *l*s and his brother put an *r* into execution.'

'Like exercution?'

'Yes. Of course the misspelling of the judge's name on the envelope could well have been a deliberate mistake.'

'When will you be seeing Peter Duxbury?'

'Seven o'clock this evening in the presence, at his insistence, of Mr Japp QC, the head of his Chambers.'

Rosa was thoughtful for a while. 'I suppose it could be someone taking advantage of what happened in court last Thursday to pursue his own vendetta or merely to play a practical joke. Thursday's events would have provided him with a ready-made smokescreen.'

'I hope you're not right as it would widen my enquiry further than I want.'

'May I ask who else apart from Pashley's relatives and my counsel is in the frame?'

'Judge Kilby is feuding with her landlord and wrote him a letter that day which she thinks might have stung him into foolish action.' He got up. 'It's been nice talking to you, Miss Epton, and thank you again for agreeing to see me.'

'I'm afraid I've not helped you very much.'

Alan Chantry smiled. 'At the moment I'm not sure whether you have or not. Between you and me, I doubt whether we'll ever be able to prove who sent the letter and, fingers crossed, the threats will fade with the passage of time.'

Rosa accompanied him to the door and they shook hands.

'I've got a telex for you,' Stephanie announced as soon as she knew Rosa's visitor had gone. 'I'll bring it along.'

There was only one person who ever sent Rosa telexes and that was Peter Chen, a Hong Kong born solicitor who had a small élitist practice in London that had him swanning round the world half the time on behalf of wealthy clients. His work couldn't be more different from Rosa's whose cases rarely took her more than a busride away from the office. They had known each other for nearly two years and she had recently been seeing him quite a lot.

He had flown to New York three days earlier and had said he would let her know as soon as he got home.

The door opened and Stephanie dashed in, dropped the telex on Rosa's desk and dashed out again, saying she could hear the phone making demanding sounds.

Rosa picked up the piece of paper and read it. 'Returning Thursday,' it ran, 'See you for dinner and love Peter.'

Either a word had got left out . . . or, then again, perhaps it hadn't. At all events Rosa knew that she looked forward to dinner and whatever with Peter on what was now the next day.

CHAPTER 6

When Celia Kilby arrived at her friend's flat for bridge on Thursday evening, she was surprised to have the front door opened by Adèle Spicer herself. Usually a grey-haired woman in a shiny black dress and with a permanently disapproving expression was hired to attend to the domestic needs.

'Mrs Smith not here this evening?' Celia enquired as she stepped past her hostess who was peering up and down the carpeted corridor outside.

'Yes, she's in the kitchen,' Adèle said vaguely. 'But I thought you might be bringing your minder, dear, and I'd better let you in myself.'

'My minder?'

'Isn't that what they're called? You know, the person who's meant to be protecting you.'

'Well, really!' Celia exclaimed in mild exasperation. 'There's probably an officer somewhere about, but I'm not on a lead if that's what you were expecting.'

'She's alone,' Adèle announced, as they entered the room where the two men were waiting.

'I'm sorry if I've let you all down,' Celia said with a brittle laugh. 'But the whole thing's become too absurd for words.

31

Every judge receives anonymous letters at some time or another. It's one way that anguished litigants or defendants can let off steam.'

'How much longer are the police going to provide you with protection?' Giles Crowhurst enquired as he came across and gave her a light kiss on the cheek.

'I've no idea. What I do know is that I'm not having anyone trailing me down to Sussex when I go there this weekend. I shan't tell the police I'm going away.'

'I don't think you should take risks, dear,' Adèle said.

'Think how it would disrupt our bridge evenings if you didn't come back,' Norman Ackroyd remarked in a jaunty tone.

Celia Kilby frowned. It was for her, not others, to make light of her situation.

'It's high time the police found out who did it,' Adèle observed with a suitable note of indignation. 'Do they have any clues?'

'I gather their enquiries are still proceeding.'

'Another way of saying they don't have a clue,' Giles remarked. 'But I agree with Adèle, I don't think you should run any risks. It's not fair on yourself, or, for that matter, the police. Not to mention your friends.'

'Thank you for your solicitude, Giles, even if not everyone would share it. Anyway we're here to play bridge, not brood over what fate may hold in store for me. Shall we begin?'

The other three followed her obediently to the table that was set up for play.

Celia now wished that she hadn't called Adèle the previous evening and told her that she was under police protection, but she had thought it right to do so at the time. She ought to have known that Adèle would be bound to gild the lily. She had given short enough shrift to Giles Crowhurst when he had phoned to express concern about her safety, having heard about the threatening letter she'd received from one of his journalist acquaintances. She had told him he spent too much time drinking in Fleet Street pubs.

They reached the table and cut for partners. Celia found

herself playing with Giles which didn't please her too well, particularly after they had lost the first rubber due to a bad call on his part.

'You'd better take a refresher course,' she said tartly, as Adèle shuffled the cards for the next hand.

'Even Homer can nod occasionally,' Norman Ackroyd said peaceably.

'As long as it is only occasionally,' Celia retorted.

Giles himself refrained from either apology or explanation, but sat looking tense and uncomfortable.

When they broke for refreshment around ten o'clock, Adèle billowed out of the room to return a couple of minutes later with plates of canapés. She was followed by the austere figure of Mrs Smith bearing a silver tray on which were set a Georgian coffee pot and creamer and four Dresden coffee cups and saucers.

'Everyone help themselves,' Adèle said, showing the way. She turned to Celia. 'Tell me, dear, whereabouts in Sussex are you going for the weekend?'

'Near Horsham.'

'Staying with friends, I expect.'

'Yes.'

'It's a lovely part of the country, especially at this time of year. So green and lush.'

From this pastoral note, the conversation moved to a libel case currently being tried in the High Court in which a titled lady was suing a gossip columnist for suggesting that she had more lovers than a busy street-walker had men in the course of a year. Adèle had been hopeful that either Celia or Giles would be able to regale her with spicy details that the newspapers had left out. She was crestfallen to discover that in fact she knew more about the case than they did.

The last rubber finished shortly after eleven-thirty and ten minutes later the three guests bid Adèle Spicer goodnight and departed.

Celia offered Giles a lift to Wimbledon main-line station from where he had a choice of trains back into central London.

It was a long-established precedent which she would like to have broken, but didn't know how to without unnecessarily hurting him.

There was an officer sitting in a car outside Adèle's block of flats and Celia went over to inform him of the detour she'd be making on her way home.

'You seem to go down to Sussex a lot these days,' Giles remarked when they were in the car. 'I didn't know you had friends there.'

'There's no earthly reason why you should know. I'm not accountable to you for my comings and goings.'

'Of course not. I was only trying to show an interest. We've known one another so long, I thought I knew where most of your friends lived.'

'But apparently not; so let's keep it that way.'

After dropping him at the station, she headed thankfully for home. Giles, she reflected, was like a burr that sticks to one's clothes. Although his company had become less and less agreeable to her, she didn't know how to shake him off. Their weekly bridge four was the main obstacle and she didn't see why she should give that up simply to avoid seeing him. The truth was that he had become a positive irritant in her life ever since she had met Edward Maxwell.

Edward was everything Giles was not, being effectual in all he undertook. Though now officially retired, he still maintained business interests that required him to visit interesting places at their best time of year. A widower in his mid-sixties he lived in quiet comfort in a charming farm-house in Sussex, where he was looked after by a married couple who had their own flat over the converted stables.

He and Celia had known each other for several months and been conducting a highly discreet affair for the past two. They were both determined to avoid any scandal and consequently kept out of one another's lives save when together in Sussex. They only ever met in the sheltered privacy of his home. On those occasions neighbours were never invited in, nor invitations to other people's houses accepted.

She was reflecting on this as she drove home. She hated to

34

have to admit to herself that her life was not as neat and clinically well-ordered as she presented it to the world. But at least the veneer of total respectability was securely in place.

While Celia Kilby's bridge quartet had been in action, Rosa had been having dinner with Peter Chen. For once he hadn't taken her to one of his favourite Chinese restaurants, but to a new French one in Chelsea which had the financial backing of one of his clients. It had a *fin de siècle* décor with artful modern lighting.

They were given a table against the wall with a semi-circular banquette seat. It was both comfortable and cosy.

'His Excellency has instructed me that you are to be his guests tonight,' the maître d' said as they sat down. 'On His Excellency's further instructions, I have put a bottle of Dom Pérignon on ice.'

'Who's His Excellency?' Rosa enquired as the maître d' went off to fetch the champagne.

'He's my client. He's an oil sheikh with a name that stretches from here to the Persian Gulf. But he's known as Brutus to his friends.'

The champagne arrived and they raised their glasses to one another.

'I think we should also drink a toast to Brutus,' Rosa said. 'Then tell me about your trip to New York.'

Peter made a deprecating grimace. 'It would have been better if you'd been there with me.'

'In what capacity?' Rosa asked lightly.

'Companion.'

'Well, next time one of your clients says come to New York and bring a companion, let me know. Incidentally I'm prepared to consider other cities as well.'

Peter gave her one of his seraphic smiles that made him look even younger. 'You were about to tell me in the taxi about the counsel you briefed who got boxed out of the ring by that old ratbag.'

'Why do you call her an old ratbag? In fact, she's rather an elegant woman.'

'Whatever she looks like, she's a ratbag underneath.'

'How do you know?' Rosa asked with an amused smile.

'I came across her once while she was still at the Bar. She treated me as if I was a coolie. Anyway, what happened in your case?'

Rosa told him as they sipped champagne and nibbled at crudités. She broke off while he ordered. *Asperges au beurre fondu*, followed by poached Scotch salmon with new potatoes and a cucumber salad and finally a raspberry soufflé. She always let him choose for her when they went to a Chinese restaurant and she was content to do so here. By now he was aware of most of her likes and dislikes where food was concerned.

When she had finished telling him what had happened in court and subsequently, he said, 'He sounds a proper wimp. The Bar seems to attract them.'

'I'm not sure that's fair.'

'It's not. But if anyone has wimpish qualities, the Bar brings them out.' He became thoughtful. 'I wonder who did send the judge that letter. It's more subtle than most. I'm glad it wasn't sent to me.'

'But if somebody is seriously minded to kill Judge Kilby, he'd hardly give advance notice.'

'Unless he wanted her to sweat a while.'

'It'd take more than that to make Celia Kilby sweat. There's nothing wimpish about her.'

'I think the police are right to take the matter seriously.'

'They didn't have any choice.'

'Probably not, but I'd still sooner be in my own shoes than in Judge Ratbag's.'

'I'll soon begin to think you're part of the plot.'

'It's just that I have a feeling and you know what we orientals are when it comes to sixth senses.'

Rosa laughed. 'With you it's a case of the thought being the father of the wish.'

Peter Chen gave a small shrug and said abruptly, 'Let's talk about something else.'

'You haven't really told me anything about your trip to New York.'

'I thought about you a lot of the time. Did you miss me?'

'It's nice to have you back,' Rosa said, sidestepping a direct answer.

'Why don't we go on holiday together later this year?'

'Where to?'

'Don't be so practical before we've reached an agreement in principle.'

Rosa was about to make a teasing reply, but realised it would annoy him.

'I've no idea when I'll be able to get away. Robin always takes August off to fit in with the school holidays. I usually wait till the summer rush is over.'

'That's all right. We can go away in late September or October. I can pick my own time.' He suddenly grinned. 'I just hang a notice on the door and go.'

'I need a bit of time to think things over, Peter. You've taken me by surprise.'

'You'd either like to go away with me or you wouldn't.'

'It's not as simple as that. But in principle it's an attractive idea.'

He let out a soft sigh. 'That's good enough for the moment.'

He didn't bring the subject up again during the rest of dinner. It was around eleven-thirty when they left the restaurant. Rosa heard him give the taxi driver his address. She felt relaxed and happy, and welcomed the arm he put around her.

He lived in a large, old-fashioned flat overlooking Battersea Gardens, which he had completely redecorated and modernised. Rosa's own tiny flat on Campden Hill in Kensington would have fitted into one of its corners.

As soon as he pulled her closer to him and kissed her gently on the lips, she knew that his telexed message from New York had meant what it said. She found herself experiencing an anticipatory tingle as the kiss continued. She had always liked Peter Chen. Soon she would discover how much she loved him.

CHAPTER 7

'You're a difficult man to get hold of, Mr Riscock,' Chief
Inspector Chantry said, as he faced the bullish figure across the
desk.

He and Detective Sergeant Kirkbride were sitting in Riscock's office in South London on the Friday of that week, it
having taken two days to arrange an appointment to see him.
He was a powerfully built man with heavy features and a pair of
eyes that were strictly for seeing with and had never been
involved in anything like a smile since they first saw the light of
day. They and a thick black moustache dominated his face.

'I'm a busy man. I can't be at everyone's beck and call,'
Riscock replied. 'Anyway, what is it you want to see me about?'

'You've no idea?'

'None.'

'I believe you own a number of properties.'

'Yes.'

'Amongst them, eight Aubusson Way in SW19.'

Riscock smiled sourly. 'So that's it! Judge Kilby's sent you
round here.'

'Did you send her an anonymous letter containing threats
earlier this week?'

'She wrote me one if you want to know,' he said angrily.

'That hasn't answered my question.'

'No, I didn't, is the answer.'

'Do you admit that you'd like to get her and the other tenants
out of the house?'

'Yes, but I can wait.'

'And you deny sending her any threats?'

'That's a load of balls.'

'What's the date on the letter she sent you which you say
contains threats?'

Riscock flicked a switch on the intercom on his desk. 'Bring
me the Kilby file,' he barked. 'On second thoughts, don't bring
the file, just tell me the date on that last letter from Judge Kilby
. . . May twenty-second . . . Thanks, sweetie.'

'I'd like you to write something down at my dictation. Will

you do that?' Chantry asked.

'Why should I?'

'To assist the police in finding out who sent threats to the judge.'

'I've already told you I didn't.'

'This could help us eliminate you from our investigation.'

'I'm not interested.'

'You mean, you won't give us your co-operation?'

'I've got more important things to do than stupid dictation.'

'Is that final?'

'Absolutely.'

'You realise that your refusal may tell against you?'

'Look, Chief Inspector, neither you nor Judge Kilby nor anyone else can frighten me. I conduct my business my own way and I don't like being messed around. Her Honour may think that just because she's a judge, she knows all the answers, but it doesn't follow. Now, I have to go out. . .'

He got up and opened his door, so that Chantry and Kirkbride had little option but to depart.

'We may want to see you again, Mr Riscock,' Chantry said as they reached the door.

'Next time make an appointment with my solicitor.'

Chantry and Kirkbride were silent until they were back in their car, then Chantry said, 'The question is, why did he refuse to co-operate? Was it guilt or natural bloody-mindedness?'

After his visitors' departure, Riscock stood deep in thought staring out of the window at a giant hoarding extolling the joys of a new deodorant. He had known perfectly well why the police had wanted to see him and felt pleased with the way he had handled the interview. He had given nothing away and had shown that their investigation held no fears for him.

He had always been quick to exploit a situation and he now wanted to survey his options.

Cedric Duthie was a model prisoner. He kept in with the staff by always doing exactly as he was told and he carefully avoided the known trouble-makers amongst his fellow inmates. He knew that if he behaved himself he had every chance of an early transfer to one of the open prisons with a more liberal regime.

Meanwhile, however, he was making the best of life in overcrowded Wormwood Scrubs. He always spent his first few days inside looking for a compatible spirit with whom he could strike up a friendship. Somebody to talk to during exercise and recreation periods.

On this occasion he had found a friend almost at once. One Percy Baker, who was near enough the same age and in for what he referred to as a bit of harmless burglary.

It was on that same Friday when Duthie and Baker were walking round the exercise yard together that Duthie suddenly heard Judge Kilby's name mentioned by the prisoner immediately in front of him, whom he knew to be Patrick Pashley. They'd arrived together from the same court on the same day.

'Women shouldn't be allowed to become bleeding judges,' Pashley was saying to his companion. 'Fancy being put inside by a woman! That really gets up my nose.' He lowered his voice so that Duthie had difficulty in hearing what came next. But he caught, 'Her turn's coming all right . . .' when, in his eagerness, he trod hard on Pashley's heel and received a stream of invective that caused him to drop hastily back a few paces.

He had heard enough, however, to know where his duty lay.

Two afternoons a week somebody, known to one and all as Mr Smithers, attended the office of Snaith and Epton to cost briefs and arrange for their taxation by the appropriate court. He was elderly and resembled a prototype cost clerk even to a pair of gold-rimmed spectacles. He was both reliable and efficient and he saved the firm's two partners an immense amount of work and hassle.

He had nearly finished his work that Friday afternoon and would be ready to leave as soon as he had checked a small detail with Rosa concerning the Duthie brief.

He knocked on her door and entered.

'May I trouble you a moment, Miss Epton?' he said. 'You recall the case of the Queen against Cedric Duthie that was dealt with last week?' He never failed to give Her Majesty a mention when referring to criminal trials.

'I certainly do, Mr Smithers, what's the query?'

He handed the brief to Rosa, who was about to open it when her eye caught counsel's endorsement of the result on the back sheet.

For a moment she felt as if Mr Smithers had given her a karate chop. Peter Duxbury had endorsed the brief correctly in every way, save that he had spelt the judge's name Kilbey.

CHAPTER 8

DCI Chantry had been summoned by the Deputy Assistant Commissioner to present himself at ten o'clock on Monday morning and report on the progress of his enquiries.

'So the answer's not very much,' the DAC observed through a cloud of pipe smoke when Chantry finished.

'I'm afraid not, sir.'

'I never held out much hope of the lab. being able to help over the hand-writing. If one of the putative suspects had obliged by misspelling the judge's name for you, that might have been significant. But printed capitals made with a ballpoint don't usually reveal any helpful characteristics, particularly if the person who did write the letter adopts a whole different style to throw us off his scent. Always assuming, that is, he's one of the people you've interviewed.' The DAC blew out another cloud of smoke. 'What about the man Riscock?'

'He's a tough property developer, sir. I suspect it's his nature not to co-operate with police.'

'Got a record, has he?'

'A conviction of GBH twenty years ago.'

'Obviously, one of the artful ones.' The DAC laid down his pipe and fixed Chantry with a hard stare. 'The sharp-ended question, Alan, is how much longer do we go on providing protection for the lady?'

'If I had my way, I'd withdraw it immediately, sir. I found out this morning that she went away at the weekend without notifying us. If she doesn't want to play fair with us, I don't see why we should continue giving her protection.'

41

'Hmm! Any idea where she went?'

'None. Apparently slipped away after telling the officer on duty she wouldn't be going out all day.'

'And he didn't see her leave?'

'He was having a tea break with the cook next door. At least I assume it was then that she skipped off.' Chantry assumed a rueful expression. 'It wasn't until she returned home last night that anyone realised she'd been away.'

'Didn't the officer on duty on Saturday night get suspicious when her flat remained in darkness?'

'There are lights operated by a time-switch when she's out at night.'

The DAC sighed. 'I'm not condoning what she did, going off like that, but we'd have had something worse than egg on our faces should anything have happened to her.'

'I realise that, sir. But she's shown a lack of co-operation all along. I had to promise that any protection we mounted would be unobtrusive. She just didn't want to know.'

'That doesn't really excuse what happened.'

DCI Chantry felt riled. 'I would suggest, sir, that she showed total irresponsibility in misleading the officer about her movements.'

'I agree,' the DAC said in a mollifying tone. 'So back to my question, how much longer are we going to provide her with so-called protection?'

'Another week, sir?'

'Any particular magic about a week?'

'In my view, the risk to her diminishes with each day that passes. More and more it seems likely that the letter was merely meant to scare her and there was never any intention of carrying out the threat.'

'In fact, you're saying it was a hoax.'

'Yes, sir.'

The DAC nodded. 'You'd better go and see her, Alan, and tell her what we have in mind.' He smiled dreamily. 'You can also castigate her for going away without warning us. It'll be a change for a police officer to reprimand a judge. It's an opportunity not to be missed.'

'Yes, sir,' Chantry replied, though with a notable absence of enthusiasm.

CHAPTER 9

Rosa had spent the weekend wondering what she should do, following her discovery of counsel's misspelling of Judge Kilby's name. She would normally have sought Robin's advice, but he and his wife had gone off on Friday afternoon to attend a wedding in Cornwall and weren't due home until late on Sunday night.

And Peter Chen, barely back from New York, had flown over to Paris to confer with a client and wouldn't be back until Monday afternoon.

The net result was that she felt abandoned at a moment of need.

As she swept and cleaned her flat on Saturday morning she pondered the moral dilemma that faced her. It continued to nag her when she went to the supermarket in the afternoon and Saturday evening's television brought no relief either. She was thankful that she was due to spend Sunday with a newly-wedded girlfriend who lived in Hampstead and whose husband was away on a business trip. Sarah was one of her few close friends and an exhilarating companion.

In the event, however, even as she listened to her friend amusingly listing the pros and cons of her newly-acquired state, Rosa's mind kept on returning to the brief with the significantly misspelt name.

By the time Sunday evening arrived, she was still trying to rationalise the situation. If Peter Duxbury had sent the letter, it could only have been done as a gesture of frustration and without any intention of carrying out the threat it contained. She could therefore keep the knowledge to herself. It would probably be a good idea if she destroyed the brief as soon as possible, as its very existence was an embarrassment.

She assumed that Chief Inspector Chantry had obtained a sample of counsel's hand-writing when he interviewed him and on that occasion Peter Duxbury must have spelt the judge's name correctly. Otherwise Chantry would have been back in a flash asking to see the endorsement on the brief.

After further mental wrestling, however, she felt she needed more information before deciding what action to take. Procrastination had its attractions. Meanwhile, she reflected wryly, she would fetch herself a drink to celebrate her failure to reach any conclusion.

She was pouring herself a glass of white wine when the telephone rang. She hoped it might be Robin, having got home earlier than expected, calling to find out if the office had collapsed following his early departure on Friday afternoon.

But the voice on the line was not Robin's.

'Miss Epton? This is Peter Duxbury. I'm sorry to bother you at home, but I'm going to be heavily engaged all tomorrow and thought I'd try and reach you before the weekend went the way of all good things. I found your number in the directory.' Rosa listened with a sinking heart to this preamble and wondered what on earth was to come. 'You remember that case before Judge Kilby?' he went on.

Had he really said *remember*? Rosa was too stunned to make immediate reply.

'I do, indeed,' she said, recovering herself.

'I'd like to borrow back my brief. I wrote a telephone number somewhere on the papers and can't now recall it. Would it be all right if I dropped in at your office first thing tomorrow morning and picked it up? I'll be passing nearby on my way to Chambers.'

'Don't bother to do that,' Rosa said, marvelling at his effrontery, 'I'll look through the brief and phone you in Chambers if I find the number you want.'

He sounded taken aback, but only momentarily. 'I don't want to give you that trouble, Miss Epton. It'll be best if I drop by and pick up the brief.'

'In that event you won't need to take the brief away with you,' Rosa said firmly. 'You can look through it at my office.'

'Yes, I suppose I could do that,' he said in a doubtful voice. Then after a pause: 'Yes, fine, I'll do that. Perhaps you'd leave it with your reception. No need to bother you personally on a

44

busy Monday morning.' He let out a small, false laugh, which Rosa assumed was meant to appease her. He seemed to have something further to say and Rosa waited. 'Incidentally, the police came to see me about some threatening letter the judge had received. Have they by any chance visited you as well?'

'Yes.'

'Ah! I don't suppose you were able to help them any more than I was?'

'Surely the officer told you why he wished to see you?' Rosa said with a touch of impatience. 'Didn't he mention that a reporter had overheard a remark you made just after the judge had left the Bench?'

'Yes, there was a reference to some such piece of nonsense. We all know that reporters are renowned for getting things wrong. It comes from continually picking up fag ends. Anyway I must ring off now, Miss Epton. Tell your receptionist I'll look in between nine-thirty and ten.'

Rosa felt that the dilemma facing her had suddenly become more acute as a result of Peter Duxbury's call. Surely he hadn't seriously thought she would be taken in by such speciousness. And yet presumably his self-assurance had led him to believe that she really would fall for his story of a telephone number written on one of the pages of his brief. She could only conclude that he had subsequently learnt the correct spelling of Judge Kilby's name and wanted to destroy any evidence that might tell against him, for she was now certain that once he got his hands on the brief it would disappear – or, if not disappear, become damaged so that its endorsement was forever illegible.

At eleven o'clock she phoned Robin's home and to her enormous relief found that he was there.

'We got back about fifteen minutes ago. Susan's upstairs unpacking while I'm recovering with a drink.'

'How was the wedding?' Rosa enquired dutifully.

'Oh, all right. Susan felt the journey was worth it, though I could have done without all that driving, with gales and deluging rain the other end. The marquee in which the reception was held almost had lift-off. But what's happened for you to call me at this hour?'

Rosa told him. 'So what do you think I ought to do when

45

Peter Duxbury calls at the office tomorrow morning?'

'It's quite a prickly one, isn't it?' Robin observed thoughtfully. 'As far as tomorrow goes, you can always make an excuse for not letting him see the brief. Say that our venerable cost clerk took it home for the weekend or it's already been forwarded for taxation. The more difficult question is what to do in the long-term.'

'As I see it, Robin, I'm not under any duty to volunteer information to Chief Inspector Chantry. On the other hand I couldn't conceal what I know if he asked me the direct question. After all, sending a letter threatening to murder is a criminal offence and there's no professional privilege involved as Peter Duxbury isn't a client.'

'I think that's a tenable position for the time being,' Robin said, 'but what happens should an attempt be made on Judge Kilby's life and the police become anxious for information from whatever source?'

'Surely we can deal with that possibility if and when it arises, and not before. Anyway, it won't arise. The letter was obviously a hoax, whoever sent it.'

'Let's hope so. Nevertheless, I think we ought to be prepared for the ultimate possibility.' He paused. 'Before Duxbury comes tomorrow morning, it'd be as well to find out whether he did record a telephone number anywhere on the brief.'

'He didn't.'

'How do you know?'

'Because between his calling me and my calling you, I drove down to the office and checked. I brought the brief back with me.'

'I suggest you keep it at home. Apart from anything else, you can tell Duxbury with a clear conscience and a straight face that you can't find it in the office.'

'That's very cynical, Robin.'

'It's the effect of drink on top of driving two hundred and fifty miles. But, seriously, I don't feel we owe Master Duxbury any favours. Rather the other way round.'

'He's clearly desperate to get hold of the brief,' Rosa remarked, 'and there can only be one explanation. He knows it incriminates him.'

46

Chief Inspector Chantry's appointment to see Judge Kilby was for five-thirty on Monday evening.

He had phoned the court immediately after his interview with the DAC and been told to come then.

'Don't arrive before half-past five,' the judge had said. 'By then the building will be near enough empty and you won't be seen by a lot of inquisitive eyes.'

His instructions were to come to the judges' entrance at the side of the building and she would arrange for him to be admitted.

When he arrived he found an unmarked police car parked on a double yellow line outside with a bored-looking officer sitting at the wheel.

'Are you waiting to drive the judge home?' he asked through the driver's window.

'Mind your own business, mate, or I'll start asking you a few questions.'

Chantry smiled in a not too friendly fashion and went on to explain his business. The officer made an embarrassed grimace and muttered a grudging apology.

Chantry walked across the pavement and rang the bell. The door was opened by Stephen Hicks, the clerk of the court, who greeted him as if they were fellow conspirators in some shady enterprise.

'Judge Kilby's in her room,' he said, after quickly closing the outside door. 'How's your investigation going?'

'It's not. There's very little more I can do for the moment.'

'Anonymous letters are best ignored in my view,' the clerk remarked in an ingratiating tone.

'Surely not when they contain threats to murder?'

'Of course that makes a difference,' he said hastily. 'Not that I think the writer of the one sent to the judge ever had any serious intention. He just wanted to worry her.'

'Is there anyone on your staff who might have written it?'

The clerk looked startled. 'Oh, I'm sure not,' he said, shaking his head vigorously.

'I have the impression that the judge isn't a particularly

well-loved figure. Has anybody here ever murmured threats against her?'

'Absolutely not.'

'After all,' Chantry went on, 'those who have to work with her every day are most likely to fall under her lash.'

'It's true we've all suffered from time to time,' Mr Hicks said with a sigh. 'I suppose Mrs Peters, the usher, is the most frequent target of Her Honour's displeasure. The judge is always finding fault with her. Either she's causing a distraction by moving about or being an annoyance by staying put in one place. She's a nice woman, but not terribly bright. I'm quite sure she would never have sent that letter. In fact, it's unthinkable. Moreover, she knows very well how to spell the judge's name.'

'Anyone else here who might have wanted to get his own back on the judge?'

'Nobody. At least, nobody who'd have gone to those lengths,' he said firmly.

They arrived outside the judge's door and the clerk knocked.

'Detective Chief Inspector Chantry,' he announced, with the air of a well-trained butler, before retreating.

Judge Kilby had disrobed and was sitting at her desk. She was wearing a black dress with an emerald green motif. Her cool poise reminded Chantry of a high-powered business executive he had once interviewed. Both women gave the impression of chic femininity combined with steely toughness.

'What do you have to report, Chief Inspector?' she enquired as soon as he was seated. 'Not very much I gather?'

He related the result of his investigation to date and went on, 'It's possible, of course, that the writer of the letter is somebody far removed from the people I've seen. Do you have any further ideas about who it might be?'

'I still believe it's somebody connected with the Pashleys. I never seriously thought it was my landlord, unpleasant person that he is. Nor did I believe it was the incompetent young counsel who represented Duthie.' She paused and carefully removed a small thread from her sleeve. Without looking up, she continued, 'So what are you proposing to do now?'

48

'The main question is how much longer we give you police protection. What's your view on that?'

'I can't pretend to feel under serious threat,' she remarked in a disdainful tone.

'I gathered not from the fact that you went away at the weekend without informing my officer.'

A small spot of colour appeared on her cheek.

'Yes, well, I didn't need protection where I was going,' she said stiffly.

'Nevertheless it wasn't very fair of you, madam.'

'You've made your point, Chief Inspector, there's no need to rub it in.'

Chantry felt pleasantly satisfied by her reaction. As the DAC had said, it's not often that police officers get an opportunity of putting judges in their place.

'I suggest we continue to provide you with protection for the rest of the week and withdraw it at the close of Friday. That'll allow you to make unhindered plans for the weekend.'

The spot of colour on her cheek returned, but she refrained from any of the withering comments Chantry was sure she would like to have made.

'Very well,' she said, as if spitting out a grape seed.

'Of course we can always review the situation should my enquiries warrant it.'

'What enquiries?' she asked suspiciously. 'I thought you'd reached a dead end.'

'Dead ends aren't necessarily permanent. I might get a sudden lead . . .'

'I can't see that happening.'

'Perhaps if I looked at things from a fresh angle . . .'

'There aren't any other angles,' she said abruptly. 'I'm not blaming you for your lack of success. Unless the writer confessed, it was inevitably a profitless task. And hand-writing experts like more than a few printed capitals to work on.'

'There was the misspelling of your name.'

'Probably a deliberate mistake. Anyway I agree that you should withdraw protection from Friday evening.' She stood up and held out her hand. 'I'll say goodbye, Chief Inspector.

Unless I hear to the contrary, I'll assume your investigation has died of inanition. There's no need for you to make a further personal report.'

Chantry was more intrigued than affronted by the dismissive note that accompanied the end of the interview. She clearly wanted a finish to his enquiries and didn't mind their lack of success. There aren't any other angles, she had said quickly, when he had mentioned the possibility of viewing events from a fresh standpoint. Was that because she feared he might start probing her own background for clues? Was it even possible that for some hidden, devious reason she had sent the letter to herself? No, that was too fanciful, he decided. He might as well let his investigation die a natural death.

It's doubtful whether he would have changed his view had Cedric Duthie's nugget of information ever reached him, though he would probably have felt obliged to re-question the Pashley family. As it was the prison officer to whom it had been imparted had as quickly dismissed it as another unreliable fag end of conversation. Prisoners like Duthie were given to buzzing as tirelessly as pollen-carrying bees.

Meanwhile, alone in her room, Celia Kilby stared vacantly out of the window. One thing for certain, she would not be spending the coming weekend in Sussex. Not after what had happened the previous day. She was still dazed that Edward Maxwell had reacted with such angry vigour.

She had fondly imagined that their relationship would continue along its untrammelled course until one or other of them tired of it. At the back of her mind, she acknowledged that she would be the more likely one to end it, but she'd assumed Edward would accept the situation in a quietly civilised manner.

Instead of which he had announced out of the blue that he wanted to marry her and wasn't that her desire as well?

No, it was not, she'd exclaimed, aghast at the proposal.

Thereafter he had bitterly accused her of leading him on and merely using him and his home for weekend recreation.

Celia was so outraged that it never occurred to her to say he had taken her by surprise and that she needed time to think things over.

It was a case of two intelligent adults having totally failed to understand one another. Each had been certain that the other shared his view of the relationship, when, in fact, nothing could have been further from reality.

It was fortunate that the row had come on Sunday evening, only shortly before Celia was due to drive back to London.

As she now sat staring out of the window, she sought to analyse her feelings, something she rarely did. Though she had never married, Edward Maxwell had not been the first man in her life, although it seemed likely he might be the last. She had enjoyed her weekends in Sussex and would miss them, but there was too high a price to pay. Why, she asked herself, had he spoilt everything by behaving so stupidly? She could attribute it only to male selfishness of the sort that brought so many defendants into the dock of her court.

Although upset by what had happened, her predominant feeling was one of profound exasperation.

There was, however, one consolation. Their affair had been known only to themselves, and so it must remain.

CHAPTER 11

For Rosa the week passed without further untoward event. Peter Duxbury had duly turned up at the office on Monday morning, only to depart a few minutes later empty-handed. Rosa assured him, however, that she would personally go through the brief as soon as it reached her hands and would call him at Chambers if she found any scribbled telephone number.

Duxbury was clearly put out, but could do nothing to change the situation. He told Rosa, with a fair amount of lawyer's flannel, not to trouble herself further as he now thought he might have written the number down on the back of an old envelope which he had unwittingly thrown away. Rosa affected to find this a plausible explanation and they parted company.

51

Friday afternoon arrived and she looked forward to the weekend with pleasure. She was going out with Peter Chen on Saturday and on Sunday was being entertained by her brother's American boss and his wife who were on a European vacation.

With the promise of dinner afterwards Peter had persuaded her to accompany him to a garden fête on Saturday afternoon. It was in aid of charity and organised by the Gillett Society of which he was a member and which comprised several sections of the legal profession.

Rosa would sooner have spent the afternoon pottering about at home, but Peter had bribed her with the prospect of an exotic meal at a riverside restaurant near Windsor.

Saturday afternoon turned out to be one of those rare summer days of hot sunshine tempered by a refreshing breeze.

The fête was well attended and both of them ran into people they knew. It was an ideal meeting-place for casual acquaintances. It was while they were standing in the shade of a large chestnut tree, sharing an ice-cream, that Rosa heard someone address her. She turned to find Judge Kilby at her side.

'I think I saw you in my court about two weeks ago,' she said with a small smile.

'Yes, that's right. I'm Rosa Epton of Snaith and Epton.' Rosa turned to bring Peter into the conversation, only to find that he and the ice-cream had quietly melted away.

'I seemed to recognise your companion's face,' Celia Kilby remarked sardonically.

'He's also a solicitor. Peter Chen.'

'Ah, yes, I recall him now. We met once while I was still in practice.'

'Are you a member of the Gillett Society?' Rosa enquired, breaking a silence that threatened to become uncomfortable.

'Yes, I have been for years, though not a very active one, I'm afraid. I thought I'd come along this afternoon as it's such a lovely day and I happened to be free.' She glanced at her watch. 'But I shall have to leave as I'm going out this evening.' After a pause she went on, 'I'm afraid you weren't very fortunate in your choice of counsel that day.'

'He wasn't my choice. The counsel I'd briefed was held up in another court. It's a not unfamiliar experience for solicitors,' she added wryly.

Celia Kilby nodded. 'It's too much work chasing too few people,' she remarked. 'Competent performers, that is. And I'm afraid barristers' clerks are not exactly blameless. They juggle their counsel around in an effort to please all the people all the time – and, of course, don't. But your young man was singularly inept, I thought.'

'You certainly gave him a rough ride.'

'I suppose I did. But I can't bear incompetence in my court, it wastes so much time. Did he take my strictures to heart?'

'Very much so.'

'But not enough to send me a threatening letter, I hope?' she said, with a brittle laugh.

Rosa felt her facial muscles stiffen with embarrassment, but fortunately Judge Kilby didn't seem to notice. She glanced again at her watch.

'It's time I made a move,' she said. 'I have several things to attend to before I go out to dinner. Perhaps I'll see you in my court again, Miss Epton.'

Rosa watched her walk purposefully towards the exit. It was apparent that she had come unaccompanied. Moreover, she didn't pause to speak to anyone on her way out.

Glancing about her, Rosa spotted Peter buying raffle tickets from a pretty girl.

'Traitor!' she said amiably, as she reached his side.

'I'm sorry, but I couldn't face making polite conversation with that woman.'

'She might have given you an excuse to make impolite conversation. Anyway, she's gone now. She has an evening engagement to prepare for.'

'So have we. Why don't we also leave?'

'It's only just after four-thirty,' Rosa said doubtfully. 'How are we going to fill in the time before dinner?'

'Don't ask idle questions, Miss Epton.'

Later, five hours later to be precise, Peter put on some

53

clothes and went out to buy a Chinese takeaway, while Rosa luxuriated in that delicious state between sleep and wakefulness, awaiting his return.

'You'll never be able to show your face at the Water Meadow again,' she said, when they were sitting on the bed surrounded by cartons of tasty food. 'Booking a table and not turning up will warrant banishment in their eyes.'

'You didn't mind not going, did you?'

'No, this is more fun.'

'That's all right then,' he said with a small sigh, 'because I never actually made a reservation.'

'You mean you planned all this?'

'I just played everything by ear and hoped,' he said with a disarming smile, at the same time leaning over and kissing her.

Early churchgoers were already up and about when he drove her back to her flat on Sunday morning. Also up and about was Tracy, the girl who delivered papers in Aubusson Way. When she reached number eight she always cycled down the front drive, made her delivery, and then departed by a side gate beyond the garages.

She was pedalling between rows of laurel bushes on the third phase of this routine when she spotted the body. It lay at the side of the path, partially hidden by a bush.

She was a practical child, who had just begun first-aid lessons, and she immediately dismounted to take a closer look. She saw at once, however, that not even advanced first aid would be of any use.

Celia Kilby lay face down with a red handled knife jutting out between her shoulder blades. The knife transfixed a sheet of paper on which was written in black ballpoint capitals:

EXECUTION CARRIED OUT SATURDAY 7 JUNE

CHAPTER 12

Judge Kilby had no place in Chantry's plans for Sunday. The morning would be taken up with unblocking a drain, fitting a new lock to the garage and mending the kitchen chair. His sister would cook lunch for both of them, after which he would read the Sunday papers, have a nap and wake up in time to go down to his local for an evening drink and a chat with some of the regulars.

That was the plan when he retired to bed on Saturday night, but at nine o'clock the next morning, before he'd even shaved or dressed, came the telephone call that told him of the judge's death.

He wasn't often thrown into a state of mental turmoil, but the news of her murder came as near to achieving that as anything that had happened in his career as a police officer. He realised that even if the lifting of protection and her death twenty-four hours later were no more than a chilling coincidence, he was in for an extremely uncomfortable time. But should evidence emerge which linked her death with the threat she'd received he'd be fortunate to survive with his career intact.

Twenty-five minutes later he knew the worst as he stared down at the body with the murderer's note still held in place by the knife that had killed her.

A canvas screen had been erected round the corpse and Detective Inspector Listerman, from the local CID stood beside him with pursed lips.

'We're still waiting for the pathologist and forensic people to arrive,' Listerman said. 'So far nothing's been touched. Would have to happen on a Sunday morning.'

'I gather the paper girl discovered the body?'

'Yes. Bright girl. Didn't panic, but got the people next door to phone the police.'

'What time was that?'

'Near enough eight o'clock.'

'If that obscene note is anything to go by, she was killed last night.'

'The doctor who attended and made a superficial examination thought she'd probably been dead for eight to ten hours. If you want my opinion, she'd been out for the evening, come home and put her car away and was on her way from the garage to the house when she was attacked.'

'Did anyone in the house hear anything?'

'One tenant's away, another's stone deaf and the third has a flat on the farther side and wouldn't have been likely to have heard anything. That's a Miss Cherry. She went to bed at ten-thirty and was unaware of what had happened until we rang her doorbell this morning. She lives on the ground floor of the house.'

'It shouldn't be difficult to trace the judge's movements yesterday evening,' Chantry observed. 'Has anyone been into her flat yet?'

DI Listerman shook his head.

A black patent leather handbag lay about a foot away from the body and Chantry bent down and opened it, taking care not to smudge any fingerprints it might have on its surface. He extracted a bunch of keys.

'Think I'll go and take a look at her car first. You'd better come, too. Somebody can let us know if the pathologist arrives.'

DI Listerman, who was on the verge of retirement and lived only for a quiet life, was content to let Chantry take charge, although strictly speaking it was, in the first instance, a matter for the local station. But he could recognise a troublesome case when he saw one and was willing to allow somebody else to put his head on the chopping block.

The garages, four of them in a row, were located about fifty yards from the house.

'Which is hers, I wonder?' Listerman said.

'She lives in flat two, so let's try garage number two.' One of the keys on her ring fitted the lock and the door opened. 'This is definitely her car,' Chantry said, as they looked at a grey Volkswagen Scirocco.

The driver's door was locked and he realised he'd not seen any car keys in her bag. Perhaps she hadn't been out in the car after all. He peered through the window at the milometer. It showed a journey of 7.4 miles, for what that was worth.

'I think I'll go and take a look around her flat,' he said. 'Apart from anything else, we need to find out who's her next of kin.'

'I'd have thought you'd have known,' Listerman said with a touch of superiority.

'Why on earth should I?'

'As part of your earlier investigation. Who to get in touch with if somebody picked her off.'

'I'm sure she'd have found that most reassuring.'

Listerman shrugged. 'It's what's happened,' he said brutally. 'I can't say I envy you.'

'I mayn't even be put in charge of the investigation.'

'Oh, you will be. Our big white chiefs at the Yard will regard it as a sort of battle course for you.'

Chantry concluded that the local DI had been miffed at not being involved in the original enquiry. There was always a bit of latent jealousy between Yard officers and those out at divisional stations and he saw Listerman's attitude in this context. Also the DI had seen younger officers overtake him and had joined the jaded ranks of time-servers.

As they returned along the path, a young detective constable ran up and announced that the pathologist had arrived.

Dr Philip Hurtmore was an eminent pathologist on the Home Office panel who turned out uncomplainingly, day or night and in all weathers, to examine corpses in situations both natural and bizarre.

'Morning gentlemen,' he said zestfully as he pulled on a pair of plastic gloves. 'All mine, is she? Taken your pictures, have you?'

'Forensic haven't come yet,' Chantry said. 'And the photographer's still around awaiting your instructions.'

'Excellent.' He bent over the body and carefully removed the knife from Celia Kilby's back. After a thoughtful pause, during which he stared from the knife to the wound and back again, he said, 'I'd say she was stabbed with considerable force, that the knife was then pulled out and reinserted in the existing wound through this sheet of paper. Where's the scene of crime officer?'

'Here, sir. Detective Constable Acott.'

'Right. Got all your little polythene bags ready?'

'Yes, sir.'

57

'Good lad. Mind how you treat this then.' He handed over the bloodstained piece of paper. 'Should be enough on that to keep a dozen experts busy,' he observed cheerfully. Holding the knife with equal care, he went on, 'There's hardly a kitchen knife on the market that can't be used murderously. You'll be lucky if you can trace the murderer through this. Hundreds must be sold every day and at Christmas time thousands. Makes a lovely present for Auntie Gwen, provided Uncle Reg doesn't harbour a wish to do her in.'

Chantry bent down and picked up the handbag gingerly by its handle. Opening it, he peered once more at its contents. There was a small diary in one of the interior pockets and he took it out.

At the same moment, Dr Hurtmore exclaimed, 'Here's a clue for you. Got her car keys beneath her hand.'

Chantry reflected that it wasn't much of a clue, but it at least solved one small mystery. She must have had the keys in her hand when she was struck down from behind. It showed she had used her car on Saturday evening.

Moving a few yards away from the scene of increasing activity, he opened the diary at Saturday, 7th June.

'Three-thirty Gillett Society fête,' he read. Beneath this entry appeared another, 'dinner with A'.

He had never heard of the Gillett Society, but there would be time enough to remedy his ignorance. He was much more interested in the dinner date with A. Who was A and where had they dined?

He flicked back through pages for June and May. The most frequent entry was 'Court', which didn't require explanation. He noted that 'bridge' cropped up every Thursday, the word being followed by 'here' or 'at A's' or 'at N's', which he took to refer to the venue.

Recalling her absence from home the previous weekend, he turned to 31st May/1st June. 'At E's' was all that rewarded him. This cryptic use of capital letters was exasperating in the circumstances. Even so, it was preferable to nothing at all.

Slipping the diary into his pocket, he decided to go and examine the flat. He informed DI Listerman where he was going and set off along the path which ran between the laurel bushes. On approaching the main door of the house he heard footsteps behind and turned to find Detective Sergeant Kirkbride hurrying after him.

'Hello, Bill. You're the first bit of good news today.'

'I got a call from the duty officer, sir, and thought I'd better come along.' He grinned. 'It's got me out of mowing the lawn.'

Chantry used one of the keys to open the house door and they made their way up a broad staircase to Judge Kilby's first-floor flat.

'Probably the first thing we should do when we get inside is go down on our knees and pray for a quick break, because if we don't get one we're in for a rough time from the media and everyone else.'

'I can see it could be a bit of a bugger, sir,' Kirkbride said sombrely. 'But it's early days yet.'

'Sounds like my epitaph,' Chantry observed as they reached the landing and he introduced himself to the PC standing outside Judge Kilby's front-door.

'No wonder she didn't intend to be evicted,' Kirkbride said, as they moved from room to room. 'I wouldn't mind swapping my semi-detached for this. Must have cost a packet to decorate and furnish.'

Chantry merely grunted. He wasn't in the mood to admire anything. The stark reality of what had happened totally occupied his mind.

Next to the spacious drawing-room was a narrow, elongated room that served as a study and it was here that he decided to concentrate his efforts, leaving Kirkbride to examine the remaining rooms.

The fourth wall of the study was a large window looking out over the garden. The judge's desk was pushed up against the window with an electric typewriter and two cardboard folders resting on it. He recalled having noticed a typewriter in her room at the court. Presumably she was someone who preferred typing to writing.

He picked up the top folder which was labelled, 'Correspondence with Landlord'. Opening it, he saw that the most recent

59

letter was the carbon of her letter dated 22nd May to Bernard Riscock. He didn't appear to have replied – unless the knife in her back had been his response.

The second folder was labelled 'Miscellaneous Correspondence', and lived up to its name. There were letters between herself and the Electricity Board about a disputed bill, to the laundry about a torn sheet and to a well-known store with an allegation of deteriorating service, which they denied with pained dignity. To the right of the desk was a filing cabinet containing further folders, relating to business and professional affairs.

Chantry wondered why the two files which were on the desk had not been put away. Perhaps she'd been intending to write a further uncompromising letter to Bernard Riscock and had got out the file in readiness.

Later he might have to examine the files in detail in a search for clues, although he hoped that wouldn't be necessary. For the moment all he need do was note the address of her bank which was the Wimbledon branch of the Southern Counties Bank and that of her solicitors who were Maurice Bleck and Co, with an office off the Strand.

It was three o'clock the next morning before Chantry got home. By then the investigation was well under way, but showing unmistakable signs of being a marathon rather than a quick sprint.

By eight o'clock he was back at the incident room he had established at the nearby divisional headquarters.

He made an appointment for later in the day to see Mr Percy Bleck, the partner in Maurice Bleck and Co who handled Judge Kilby's affairs. He had with difficulty traced the solicitor to his home in Hertfordshire on Sunday evening, but found him tiresomely uncommunicative. He had certainly been shocked by news of his client's demise, but at the same time had sounded mysteriously ill at ease.

He had been reviewing overnight developments, or rather the lack of them, when he received a call from the clerk at Judge Kilby's court.

'Certain information has just come into my possession that I feel I must pass on to you at once,' Mr Hicks said portentously. 'Would it be convenient for you to drop by the court this morning?'

'Can't you tell me on the phone?'

'I'd much prefer to impart it in person. You'll understand why when we meet.'

'I'll come over right away.'

'I'll be waiting for you in my office. The court's not sitting today as a mark of respect. Also there's no judge available at such short notice,' he added in case Chantry might think they had gone into deep mourning.

When he arrived at the court he was taken immediately to the clerk's personal office. Somewhat to his surprise the lady usher was also there, looking nervous and upset.

'You met Molly Peters when you were here before, I think,' Mr Hicks said.

'I don't think we were ever formally introduced,' Chantry said, giving her a quick smile. 'Mrs Peters, is it?'

She nodded and looked anxiously towards the clerk who said, 'Molly has asked me to be her spokesman. What she has to say is that on that fateful Thursday two and a half weeks ago she picked up Mr Duxbury's brief from the floor and noticed that he had misspelt Judge Kilby's name. He had put Kilbey.'

Chantry frowned. 'Picked it up off the floor, did you say?'

'That's correct. You see, the sleeve of her usher's gown had brushed it off the table and she stooped to pick it up. Mr Duxbury was speaking to his instructing solicitor at the time and probably never noticed what had happened.'

'That was on the twenty-second of May,' Chantry said, fixing the usher with a quizzical stare, 'and today is the ninth of June.'

Mr Hicks went quickly on, 'There's an explanation. As I told you last time we met, Judge Kilby was wont to vent her annoyance on Mrs Peters in a way that upset many of us who had to be in court. She had been particularly sharp with her that very day. Moreover, Mrs Peters had felt extremely sorry for Mr Duxbury whom she came to see as a fellow sufferer. At all events when the threatening letter came a few days later with the judge's name wrongly spelt, she decided, for what I

61

consider understandable reasons, not to add to counsel's troubles by telling what she knew. But now with the judge viciously murdered she realised she had a duty to speak out . . .'

Turning slowly towards the usher, Chantry said, 'Do you confirm what Mr Hicks has just told me?'

'It's the honest truth, sir. I'll swear it on the Bible.'

'Clearly it's something that could alter the course of your enquiries,' the clerk said with a certain air of relief.

Chantry nodded. 'It could even be the break I prayed for yesterday.'

CHAPTER 13

Rosa had learnt of Judge Kilby's murder on the midnight news soon after she arrived home from her day out with her brother's employer and his wife. It had been an enjoyable day in the company of two delightful and tireless Americans.

As soon as she reached the office on Monday morning she went along to Robin's room.

'No need to ask what brings you here,' he remarked. 'I did try and call you when I first heard the news, but you were apparently out.'

'I spent the day with friends of my brother's,' she said, as though that made her absence more respectable than if she had been with Peter. 'I can still hardly believe it. A judge murdered in cold blood. And to think I talked to her on Saturday afternoon.' She went on to tell Robin about the Gillett Society fête.

'I can't help wondering whether there was anything symbolic about the way she was killed,' Robin remarked.

'Stabbed in the back, you mean?'

'Yes.'

'I've wondered the same thing.'

'And what's your conclusion?'

'That only someone with a deranged mind could have been so motivated.' She pushed back her hair which had fallen forward on either side of her face. 'But leaving such a grisly possibility aside, what are we going to do about Peter Duxbury's brief? It's like a time-bomb ticking away in the office.'

'I'll try and get hold of Sam Dibden,' Robin said. 'He's always full of wise advice.'

Sir Samuel Dibden was an ex-President of the Law Society who had retired to Oxfordshire. His son, Alex, had been a friend of Robin's since their days together at university.

'More than ever,' he went on, 'I feel we must avoid obstructing the police, while at the same time not volunteering any information. That should be our holding position. Do you agree?'

'It really does look bad for Peter Duxbury,' Rosa said unhappily. 'First of all the letter containing threats, of which he was almost certainly the sender, and now the promised follow-up.'

'It's almost too straightforward.'

'Obvious answers are often the most compelling.'

'Was Duxbury at this fête on Saturday?'

'I didn't see him.'

'I just wondered if he might have bumped into Her Honour over a cup of tea and a cress sandwich?'

'I'm sure he wasn't there.' She sighed. 'I just hope we're not going to find ourselves involved.'

It seemed that the words were scarcely out of her mouth before Stephanie announced that Chief Inspector Chantry was on the line and wished to speak to her.

'I'd like to come and see you as soon as possible, Miss Epton,' he said. 'You'll have heard, of course, of Judge Kilby's murder?'

Rosa conceded that indeed she had and added that she would be in all morning.

'Perhaps it would be a good idea if we saw him together,' Robin observed.

'I think it'd be an extremely good idea,' Rosa said.

Chantry arrived thirty minutes later and lost no time in declaring the reason for his visit.

'Can you confirm, Miss Epton, that Mr Duxbury spelt Judge Kilby's name Kilbey when he endorsed his brief?'

'Yes, he did,' Rosa said. 'Though I only noticed it later.'

Chantry made a gesture that seemed to indicate he wasn't bothered about excuses.

'Do you have the brief here?'

'Yes.'

'May I see it please?'

Rosa gave Robin a helpless look.

'I'll try and find it,' Robin said, getting up and leaving the room.

While he was gone, Rosa, who was feeling as if she had just been run into by a bus, said, 'I don't know whether it's of any help, but I happened to meet Judge Kilby on Saturday afternoon at a fête I attended.'

'The Gillett Society fête?'

'Yes.'

'Did you speak to her?'

'We had a brief conversation about nothing in particular. She did mention, however, that she was going out to dinner and had to leave soon.'

'Did she say where or with whom?' Chantry asked eagerly.

Rosa shook her head. 'No.'

'Was she with anyone at the fête?'

'Not as far as I was aware. In fact, soon after we'd finished talking, I saw her leaving alone.'

'You're being most helpful, Miss Epton.'

'I'm afraid it's all rather negative.'

'As you well know, an accumulation of negatives forms a large part of any police enquiry. Was Mr Duxbury by any chance at the fête?'

'I didn't see him.'

Robin returned with the brief and handed it to Chantry who examined it with a grave expression.

'May I take possession of it?' he asked, glancing up.

'I suggest you take a photocopy of the relevant page,' Robin said. 'But I promise you the brief won't be destroyed.'

'Fair enough.' In a thoughtful tone he went on, 'Mr Duxbury has a lot of explaining to do. When I was at school two and two made four and I doubt whether he'll be able to persuade me otherwise. Well, I must be on my way, as I have a great many enquiries to make. Judge Kilby appears to have had a knack of surrounding herself with a certain amount of mystery.'

After Chantry had left, Rosa returned to Robin's room.

'I think we acquitted ourselves all right,' he remarked. 'Indeed, I doubt whether anyone could fault our performance.'

'Except, perhaps, for Peter Duxbury,' Rosa replied with obvious unhappiness.

If Mr Percy Bleck was the son of the firm's founder, then Maurice Bleck and Co. had been in business for a long time, for Chantry reckoned that the man facing him across the desk was over seventy, although a fit and well set-up septuagenerian.

'What a terrible thing to have happened,' he declared in a deep, fruity voice. 'I used not to see Judge Kilby very often, but she'd been my client for over twenty years.' In a faintly disapproving tone, he went on, 'She liked to handle a number of her legal affairs herself, but from time to time she had recourse to our expertise.'

Chantry listened to this preamble with a touch of impatience, wondering where it was going to lead. Experience told him, however, that to interrupt a lawyer usually served only to prolong matters.

But when a suitable moment came with Mr Bleck pausing to assemble his next utterance, he said quickly, 'All I really need to know at this stage is Judge Kilby's next of kin.'

'I was coming to that,' Mr Bleck said in the same measured tone. 'Whether or not it's the only thing you need to know is another matter. This may come as something of a surprise to you, but in law her next of kin is her son.'

'I never knew she'd been married.'

'She never was,' Mr Bleck said, enjoying his moment of theatre. 'At the age of nineteen she was seduced, as a result of which she gave birth to a son. The father of the child abandoned her as soon as he knew of the pregnancy. He went abroad and passed completely out of her life. Anyway, the son, Anthony, is now thirty-two. He was brought up by his maternal grand-mother, who, for a long time, he believed to be his mother, and emigrated to Australia as soon as he had finished with school. He married out there, but the marriage broke up and he recently returned to this country.'

'And he's Judge Kilby's heir?'

'I never said that. I merely said he was her next of kin.'

'So who does inherit the bulk of her estate?'

'A number of legal charities are the main beneficiaries.'

'Does her son get anything?'

'A small legacy. Five hundred pounds. But that's all.'

'I take it you learnt the family history from Judge Kilby herself?'

'Good gracious, no! From her mother who died last year. Mother and daughter never got on and old Mrs Kilby related it to me when I became her solicitor. She came to my firm shortly before her death and quite without her daughter's knowledge. As far as Judge Kilby was concerned, I was unaware of the background.'

'But the legacy to Anthony Kilby?'

'There was no reference to him as her son in the will. He was merely somebody of the same name. He could have been a distant cousin.'

'You say he's now back in this country. May I ask how you know that?'

'Because he phoned to ask me something about his grandmother's estate. He said he was back, but was unsure of his future movements.'

'Was he in touch with his mother?'

'I can't say for certain, but I suspect that he'd approached her.'

'Is he well off?'

'From the fact that he was staying at a cheap hotel in Earl's Court, I'd say not. His grandmother didn't leave a great deal. She once told me that her daughter made her what she obviously regarded as an inadequate allowance.'

'And what about Judge Kilby's estate? Is that substantial?'

'I've not yet worked out the figures, of course, but I'd say it'll come to a comfortable sum.'

Chantry digested this with a thoughtful air, then said,

'Presumably when the mother died Judge Kilby became aware that you'd been acting for her?'

Mr Bleck assumed a portentous expression. 'Yes. I explained to her that her mother had approached me and that, as there was no apparent conflict of interest, I saw no reason not to take her on as a client.'

'What was Judge Kilby's reaction?'

'I'm afraid she wasn't too pleased. Indeed, I thought she might take her business elsewhere, but she didn't. I like to think that wiser and more sensible considerations prevailed.' He stroked his chin with a gravely judicial air. 'I trust, Chief Inspector, that you will treat everything I've told you with the utmost confidence. In particular about the judge's unfortunate girlhood lapse.'

What was a lapse in those days had now become relatively commonplace, Chantry reflected. He gave an abstracted nod. He was busy wondering if the A with whom Judge Kilby had dined only a few hours before her death could be her son, Anthony. It was something he would have to find out, if only to eliminate a possible red herring.

For the moment, however, Peter Duxbury was the person on whom his sights were firmly focused.

CHAPTER 14

Giles Crowhurst was too upset by events to go into Chambers on Monday morning. He phoned his clerk to explain.

'I quite understand, Mr Crowhurst,' the clerk said. 'We're all shattered by the news of Judge Kilby's death. I know that Mr Tangley intends calling you as soon as he gets back from court.' Robert Tangley QC was head of Chambers. The clerk went on in his best bedside tone, normally reserved for mollifying solicitors, 'There's nothing urgent awaiting your attention. We'll hope to see you in a day or so.'

Giles had, as protocol required, informed head of Chambers and his clerk that he was seeking a salaried post in Brussels and his forthcoming retirement from the Bar was now common knowledge in the Temple. It was one of those supposed secrets to which everyone who cared to know was privy.

His practice was being run down in anticipation of the event, although this was little more than a polite fiction, given the paucity of his work. Nevertheless, it was a fiction that was scrupulously observed by Harry, the Chambers' clerk.

'The person I feel really sorry for,' he had remarked earlier that morning when speaking to Robert Tangley, 'is Mr Crowhurst. He'd always kept in touch with Miss Kilby since her appointment to the circuit Bench and her death must have come as a terrible shock to him. I think we all know that he still entertained hopes of marrying her.'

Tangley had fixed the clerk with a distinctly sardonic look. 'Stop sounding like an agony column, Harry. Personally, I can't imagine a worse fate than being married to Celia Kilby. Giles Crowhurst should consider himself fortunate. However, that said, let's hope he gets this job in Brussels. He needs a complete break and, nice fellow that he is, he's not a great asset to Chambers.' He turned to go. 'I'll leave you to find out the funeral arrangements. I suppose I'll have to go as the representative of her old Chambers. Mr Crowhurst will presumably attend as a personal friend of the deceased. I imagine there'll be a memorial service later when Bench and Bar can pay their corporate respects and silently note the absentees for later comment over a drink.'

Meanwhile, Giles Crowhurst was in a turmoil. His world had suddenly spun off its axis and he knew that life would never be the same again. All his friends would rally round with kind words and practical suggestions but, as with Humpty Dumpty, they wouldn't be able to put him together again.

He had been living on black coffee and cigarettes and hadn't even bothered to go to bed the previous night, sitting instead in a chair staring into dark space until first light had come and with it a few snatched minutes of uneasy sleep.

He had tried to call Adèle Spicer on Sunday evening, but had been unable to get any reply. Now, at ten o'clock on Monday morning, she phoned him.

'My dear Giles, I'm utterly distraught,' she gasped down the line. 'I was out all yesterday and only got home after midnight. It was only when I saw a paper this morning that I learnt about poor Celia. It must have been a maniac. He was obviously lurking in the bushes and jumped out at her. She never took that threat seriously enough.' The words gushed out as, striking a more practical note, she went on, 'I doubt whether we can find a suitable substitute for Celia this coming Thursday, though I'm sure it would be her wish that we continued our weekly game.'

'I couldn't possibly consider playing this week,' Giles said. 'I'm much too upset.'

'Of course, dear, but you mustn't give up living altogether. Celia wouldn't want that. Incidentally, Giles, who was it she used to visit in Sussex at weekends? She was always a bit mysterious about it, but I expect you know.'

'Well, I don't. I've no idea at all.'

'I only wondered. It's not really any of my business.'

'Nor mine.'

Nevertheless it was a question that occupied his mind after their conversation had finished. It wasn't for want of trying that he had failed to find out the nature of Celia's assignations. Or, more particularly, the identity of the other party.

Bernard Riscock regarded Judge Kilby's death with complete satisfaction. A major irritant in his life had been removed and nobody need expect to hear him expressing hypocritical sentiments about her sudden demise. It was more an event for celebration, for he now reckoned his way was clear to evicting the remaining tenants at 8 Aubusson Way. It might still take a bit of time, but they would be like a defeated army with the departure of their leader.

He realised that he would still have to contend with the police, but that wasn't a prospect which bothered him. At worst, the police had never been more than a minor irritant in his life.

Nevertheless it would be as well to ensure that his tracks were properly covered. He knew that it was the neglected detail which could imperil any enterprise and he didn't intend there should be so much as a hiccup in his plans from now on.

With the police still in mind, he decided to polish up his alibi.

Edward Maxwell had long believed that he was proof against panic. Indeed, he was renowned in many a boardroom for his nerve of steel and his carefully controlled reserves of ruthlessness.

But murder, the real thing that is, was something new in his experience and there had been moments during the past twenty-four hours when he had needed every gramme of self-discipline he could find.

His continuing strand of hope lay in the fact there was nothing to connect him with Celia Kilby. Thank goodness it had been in their common interest to behave with the utmost discretion. It was the one redeeming feature in what had turned out to be a disastrous relationship.

How on earth could he, Edward Maxwell at the age of sixty-six, have let himself become so totally infatuated? He hated any situation he couldn't rationalise and it was no comfort to attribute what had happened to his glands having a final fling. They had never led him into such difficulty before. He had learnt during the past week that infatuation was worse than any fever. The more so when you'd thought yourself to be immune.

After their stormy parting that Sunday evening, he had been torn in two directions. A wild, tormenting desire to see her again had battled with an equal determination not to be the one to extend an olive branch. But desire eventually proved the more powerful and on Tuesday he had called her. Surely she would realise he was making an amend, swallowing his pride and eating humble pie all in one? If she did, she gave no evidence of the fact and had told him coolly, but emphatically, not to call her again.

For three days he burned with further angry, resentful thoughts, unable to think of anything else. It was far worse than the severest attacks of malaria from which he had suffered.

Then on Friday his then urgent desire to see her again overwhelmed all his other feelings and he called her that evening, only to have her put down the receiver as soon as she heard his voice.

70

Once more he was filled with bitter rage. He knew he couldn't go on like this for much longer. In any event it was against his nature not to bring issues to a conclusion . . .

That had been Friday. Today it was Monday and he was thanking God there was nothing to connect him with the dead woman. Or was it more of a prayer?

When later on Monday morning Chief Inspector Chantry phoned Peter Duxbury's Chambers, he was informed by the clerk, whom he'd met on a previous occasion, that Mr Duxbury wasn't in.

'Do you have any idea when he'll be back?' Chantry enquired.

'I can't say,' the clerk replied in an evasive tone.

'Which court is he attending this morning?'

'He's not actually in court. He went away for the weekend and hasn't yet returned.'

'Do you mean he's missing?'

'No, nothing as dramatic as that. I imagine he's on his way back now. Knowing he wasn't in court today, he most likely decided to stay an extra day.'

'Nevertheless, you were expecting to see him this morning?' Chantry pressed.

'I'm sure there's a good reason for his absence, Mr Chantry.'

I'm sure there is, too, Chantry thought.

'Can you tell me where he was spending the weekend?'

'I believe he was visiting friends in North Wales, but he didn't leave an address. There was no cause for him to do so.'

'I see. And he hasn't phoned to explain why he's not back?'

'No,' the clerk said reluctantly.

'I imagine you can guess why I wish to get in touch with him?'

'Yes.'

'It would be in his best interest to contact me as soon as possible.'

'I'll certainly pass that on to him. I'm sure he has nothing to worry about.'

Unless I'm losing my marbles, Chantry thought, he has plenty to worry about.

71

CHAPTER 15

Once in a while Rosa stayed late in the office rather than take papers home to work on in the more relaxed atmosphere of her flat.

It usually happened when the case papers were too cumbersome to carry around or she needed to look up points of law in their small, but well-chosen, library which was housed in Robin's office.

She had spent the whole of Monday afternoon working on a tax fraud, but had had so many interruptions that she decided to stay on after everyone had gone and the telephone had fallen silent.

It was a case that required all her concentration if she was to understand its intricacies. It also contained several points of law that would need research among the reported cases.

About seven o'clock she went out to a nearby Italian café, where the patron and his son were, business permitting, apt to give her smacking kisses, while the patron's wife and his sister would clutch her to their bosoms as though she'd just returned from some perilous journey. After these greetings she was thankful to sit down and rest.

On this occasion only the handsome son and his mother were in the café. Rosa ordered a cheese omelette and salad, to be followed by a cassata ice-cream and a cup of coffee.

'One special cheese omelette for Signorina Rosa,' the son sang out through the hatch to a cook who was permanently out of sight, but who she presumed to be another member of the family.

Their busy time was the middle of the day, with just a few regulars appearing in the evening. Rosa recognised one old man having supper with a copy of *War and Peace* open beside him. He had been reading it for as long as she could remember.

Half an hour later, fortified by her meal, she made her farewells (she might have been a favourite daughter leaving home for ever) and returned to the office. She reckoned that, provided her spirit didn't cave in, three hours' concentrated work would see her mastery of the case.

It was shortly after eleven o'clock when she decided to pack up and go home. At least she now had the satisfaction of understanding the case, which she hadn't when she'd begun. She returned the various legal volumes she'd accumulated around her to their shelves and went back to her room to tidy up the papers that covered her desk. She was glad she hadn't attempted to take them home.

She had just switched off her light when she heard a sound at the front door. Old buildings have lives of their own at night and she imagined it was a floor joist going in for a bit of nocturnal expansion or contraction. Except that it hadn't really been that sort of sound. It was more furtive and purposeful.

She paused with her hand resting on the door-knob and listened. Her ears had not deceived her. There it was again, as if somebody was trying to insert a key in the lock of their main door. The only people who had keys to the office were herself, Robin and Stephanie. It wasn't the sort of building that had a caretaker and the only other occupant was an accountant on the ground floor, who worked the shortest hours of anybody Rosa had met.

She couldn't think it was Stephanie, so it had to be Robin, who'd probably forgotten something he needed for court the next morning. Even as the thought was being registered, she heard the sound again. This time it was more a stealthy scratching noise.

More intrigued than anxious, Rosa made her way along the passage to the lobby which served as a waiting-room and where Stephanie presided on the farther side of a hatch marked 'Reception'.

Quite definitely somebody was trying to get into the office and not being very successful. It was the ineffectiveness of the attempt that decided Rosa not to phone for the police. Flashing blue lights and wailing sirens seemed rather extreme for the situation. The only alternative, however, was to fling open the door and take the would-be intruder by surprise.

On her return from the café she had merely dropped the catch and hadn't bothered to double-lock the door.

She reached the door and got ready to pull it open. There was

73

no point in shouting at whoever it was the other side, as this would only frighten him off and leave the mystery unsolved.

As she jerked the door wide open, there was a sharp cry of dismay and Peter Duxbury came catapulting into the lobby.

'Oh, my God!' he exclaimed in an anguished tone.

'I suppose I should have guessed,' Rosa said. 'So now you're also a burglar.'

'Oh, my God!' he moaned again.

'Still trying to get hold of that brief?' she said scornfully.

'Please don't send for the police. Please help me.'

'Help you!' Rosa echoed in amazement.

'The police want to interview me and I need advice. Will you act for me? Please don't turn me away.'

'You make it sound as if you're on the run.'

'I might just as well be. When I phoned my Chambers this afternoon, the clerk told me that Chief Inspector Chantry had been asking my whereabouts and leaving messages for me to get in touch with him as soon as possible. Allegedly in my own interest,' he added bitterly.

'We can't go on talking out here all night,' Rosa said, after a pause. 'We'd better adjourn to my office.' She gave him a wry glance. 'You realise, of course, that I charge double-time after midnight.' They reached her room and she said, 'You could probably do with a drink. I can offer you whisky or brandy or slivowitz which a client brought back from a holiday in Jugoslavia. Which do you fancy?'

'Whisky, please.'

As Rosa poured the drinks, she reflected on the transformation that had taken place in Peter Duxbury since their first encounter. Gone was the cocky, pompous, self-assured young man, to be replaced by someone who was bewildered and frightened and unsure of himself.

Sitting down at her desk, she said, 'You'd better select a starting point and begin. Then I'll tell you whether or not I can help you.' She frowned as she thought of something. 'Incidentally, how were you trying to get into our office?'

He gave her a shamefaced look. 'A burglar I once defended gave me a set of skeleton keys. I managed to open the downstairs street door, but couldn't find one to fit your lock. It's the first time I've ever used them.'

'All right, now begin,' she said without much encouragement in her tone.

'I was supposed to be spending the weekend with friends in North Wales, but I've been feeling so low and depressed recently I felt I couldn't face it. I just wanted to be on my own somewhere, so I drove down to Albury near Guildford where I have the use of a cottage. It belongs to an uncle who lives in Ireland and is in a pretty dilapidated state, but I have a key and go down when I want to get away from everything. There's no electricity laid on and you have to draw water from a pump. Anyway, that's where I spent the weekend, doing nothing except feeling sorry for myself. Then on Sunday evening I heard on the portable radio I always take with me that Judge Kilby had been murdered. That really threw me. I'd intended coming back to London early on Monday morning, but I just stayed on wondering what to do. Then this afternoon I drove to the nearest telephone kiosk and called Chambers and was told Chantry had been trying to get in touch with me.' He paused and gave Rosa a despairing look. When he went on it was in a tone that clearly cost him considerable effort. 'Looking back now, I realise I must have been out of my mind. My one thought was that I had to get hold of that brief . . . I imagine you know why?' Rosa nodded. 'I saw it as even deadlier evidence against me now that she's been murdered.' He let out a sigh that shook his whole body. 'God, I've been a fool!'

'You've certainly not shown much subtlety in your efforts to get your hands on the brief. In any event, you're too late. Chantry was here first thing this morning and we couldn't in the circumstances refuse him sight of it.'

'So he knows.'

'He knows that you misspelt the judge's name, but that's all he learnt here. It doesn't mean you're the only person to misspell it.' He gave Rosa a tortured look which told her there was worse to come.

'I also sent the judge that threatening letter,' he said in an exhausted whisper.

CHAPTER 16

Rosa stared in disbelief at the dejected occupant of her visitors' chair. She felt that anything she said would only add to his anguish and decided that silence would be kindest. After a moment he contributed his own comment.

'I realise I've been incredibly foolish. I can't think why I did it. It was a spontaneous reaction to the humiliation to which she'd subjected me. I just wanted to get back at her. God, how I wish I'd never posted it.'

'What made you mail it in SE7?' Rosa asked and, when he didn't reply, went on, 'Was it because you knew that Pashley came from that area?'

He closed his eyes and gave a painful nod.

Nothing very spontaneous about that, Rosa reflected. Rather a calculated determination to mislead.

He looked up suddenly and caught her gaze.

'You don't think *I* murdered her, do you?'

'Did you?'

'No,' he said, shaking his head vigorously. 'I only left the cottage once over the whole weekend. I went for a drink at the Black Swan at Chilbury. It's beyond Albury and about five miles from the cottage.'

'What time was that?'

'I arrived there about nine and stayed just over an hour.'

'So you could easily have driven up to Aubusson Way and been there by eleven,' Rosa observed in a thoughtful voice.

He frowned. 'Aubusson Way? Isn't that where Judge Kilby lived?'

'Yes. I was wondering what sort of alibi you had? Not much of one, it seems.'

'I never murdered her,' he said in a voice as taut as a piano wire. 'I only know her address because I read it in the paper this morning. You must believe me.'

'It's Chief Inspector Chantry who has to be convinced, not me. Look at it for a moment from the police point of view. Judge Kilby receives an anonymous letter threatening her with death. Two weeks later she's murdered and pinned to her body is a note referring to her execution, which was the word used in the letter.' Rosa held up her hand when Peter Duxbury seemed about to interrupt. 'And that's not all. The original letter referred to something she'd done the previous Thursday, which was the 22nd of May. No need to remind you what happened that day as far as you're concerned. We all know the judge behaved abominably towards you and unfortunately you were later heard to utter threats against Her Honour. In those circumstances it's small wonder that Chantry wants to interview you. He's investigating a murder for which he feels himself indirectly responsible, so he'll be more than usually eager to bring the case to a quick and successful conclusion.'

'What do you want me to do? Confess to a crime I didn't commit?' His tone was resentful and self-pitying.

'If that's your reaction, you might as well leave now and I can go home to bed.'

'I'm sorry. I'm upset.'

Rosa wondered if he yet fully appreciated the extent of the trouble in which he had landed himself. He had committed a criminal offence that also involved gross professional misconduct. Whether or not he ever ended up in court, he was certain to be disbarred. It was difficult to see how the effects of all his folly could be successfully mitigated.

She now went on, 'The sooner you get in touch with Chantry, the better. The question is how much to tell him. I don't believe in my clients making admissions which merely serve to help the police prove their case. On the other hand, I can't be a party to your telling him what I know from your own lips to be a lie. That means I couldn't act for you if you denied sending the threatening letter.'

'But if I tell the police I sent it, I'll be half-way to admitting murder in their view.'

'I know. That's what bothers me. It might be better if you got up and walked out of here.'

He shook his head. 'Please, Miss Epton. I need your help.'

Rosa smothered a yawn. She was feeling utterly exhausted. 'Where are you proposing to spend the night? I wouldn't be surprised if the police were keeping a watch on your home.'

'I can doss down at a cousin's flat.'

'That might be wiser. We'll meet back here at nine o'clock in the morning.'

As they both got up, Rosa noticed him blink away some tears and in that moment saw him, for the first time, as an ordinary, frail human being.

At half-past seven the next morning, she was on the phone to Robin's home. His wife, Susan, answered and almost immediately let out a cry.

'Hold on a moment,' she exclaimed before Rosa could say anything. A few seconds later she was back on the line. 'Sorry about that, but the milk was about to boil over. Who is it?'

'Rosa. You're obviously in the throes of getting breakfast,' Rosa said apologetically. 'But could I have a word with Robin?'

'I'll give him a shout. I think he's still shaving. Do you mind if I desert you meanwhile, but the children have to be at school early this morning and I have an idea that Toby's already gone back to bed. I'll call Robin now . . .'

It was about a couple of minutes before her partner came on the line.

'What's up?' he asked crisply, knowing that Rosa wouldn't be calling at that hour without good reason.

She told him what had happened the previous evening.

'If I were you, I'd only agree to represent him if he comes clean with the police. That means telling them that he was the sender of the letter.'

'It'll be the end of his career.'

'The sooner the better from what you've told me about him,' Robin said. 'He's obviously an even stupider young man than we believed, though it still seems unlikely he's a murderer. Whoever did kill the judge was clearly exploiting an existing situation. I suggest you phone Chantry and arrange an appointment for you and Duxbury to see him.'

'Thanks for your advice, Robin. Enjoy your breakfast.'

'With two fractious kids at the table, enjoy is hardly the right word.'

Rosa was glad to have had an opportunity of discussing the

issues with Robin, even if she wasn't wholly won round to his view.

Her own tranquil breakfast consisted of two cups of coffee topped with skimmed milk and a slice of wholemeal bread spread with honey.

By ten minutes to nine she was in the office awaiting Peter Duxbury's return. But when the hour passed without his appearance she began to wonder if he had had second thoughts about coming back. He had been in such an overwrought state the previous evening that he might have done anything. Suicide seemed unlikely, but simple disappearance was another matter. He was bright enough (or was he?) to remain several moves ahead of the police. If he had flown the country, Rosa hoped it would be the end of her involvement with him.

It was while she was contemplating all this that her phone rang and Stephanie announced Chief Inspector Chantry on the line.

'Good morning, Miss Epton. We've picked up Mr Duxbury and he's at the Vale police station. He's declining to answer any questions until you arrive.'

Chantry greeted Rosa with reserve when she arrived at the police station. She suspected that he felt she had pulled a fast one somewhere along the line, but that he had nevertheless managed to come out on top.

'You didn't mention that Duxbury was your client when I came to your office yesterday morning,' he said.

'That was because he wasn't. If he had been, I shouldn't have let you see the brief.'

'Oh!' He sounded taken aback. 'Well if you're ready, perhaps we can start the interview.'

'I'd like to have a few minutes alone with my client first.' When he hesitated, she added, 'It's a reasonable request.'

'All right then. A few minutes.'

Peter Duxbury was sitting in a small, cheerless room when Rosa was shown in. 'Thank God you're here,' he said.

'What happened? How'd the police find you?'

79

'I couldn't get any answer at my cousin's flat, so I decided to risk going back to my own. There must have been an officer keeping it under surveillance, because I'd barely let myself in before a fleet of police cars arrived and I was hauled off. Anyone would have thought I was the most wanted man in England.' He gave a dramatic shrug. 'But I'm past caring what happens to me now. Things can't get any worse.'

Rosa looked at him thoughtfully. 'Are you really sure you want me to act for you?'

'Absolutely sure.'

'After all,' she went on, 'you must know a great many solicitors better than you know me.'

'I know you by reputation.'

'What about your head of Chambers? He held your hand last time the police interviewed you.'

'The circumstances are quite different now. He'd have no locus. A solicitor is what I need, and I want you.'

On her way to the police station, Rosa had had time to review the advice she proposed to tender. With his arrest, circumstances had changed and she was no longer minded to advise him to admit having sent the letter. Eventually, if he was charged, he would probably have to plead guilty, but meanwhile she saw nothing to be gained in making life easier for the police. The moment would come when Chantry would ask him directly if he had written the letter and it was then that tactics would count.

A few minutes later, Detective Sergeant Kirkbride stuck his head round the door.

'Mr Chantry would like to know if you're ready?' he said in a tone that implied that 'no' would not be an acceptable answer.

Rosa nodded and they followed Kirkbride along a passage and up a flight of stairs to a room in which an edgy Chief Inspector Chantry was waiting. He would much sooner be conducting the interview without Rosa's attendance, but the recent Police and Criminal Evidence Act had contrived, as parliament had intended, to shackle the police in their interrogation of suspects. In their view, it made the nailing of suspects that much more difficult. As if, Chantry reflected, the interviewing of a member of the Bar on a serious criminal matter wasn't difficult enough anyway. It all came down to what you could get away with and he was under no illusions as to that. Nevertheless, whatever his regard for Rosa, it wouldn't prevent him outsmarting her should the opportunity arise.

The interview began on a quiet, almost conversational, note. It wasn't long, however, before he produced the photocopy of the back sheet of Peter Duxbury's brief in the case of R. *v.* Duthie.

'Is that endorsement in your handwriting?' he asked.

'Yes.'

'You spelt Judge Kilby's name with an e.'

'I know. It was a slip.'

'It was a slip you repeated when you sent her the threatening letter, wasn't it?'

'My client doesn't wish, on my advice, to comment on that,' Rosa broke in quickly.

'I'm not inviting his comment, merely an answer to my question.'

'Then I suggest you rephrase your question.'

Chantry hid his annoyance. 'Were you the person who wrote and sent Judge Kilby that threatening letter?'

'I advise my client not to answer that question.'

Studiously ignoring Rosa, Chantry fixed Duxbury with an unfriendly look.

'Did you send that letter?'

Duxbury swallowed nervously. 'I have no comment to make.'

'When did you first realise you had misspelt the judge's name?'

'I can't remember.'

'When I first interviewed you and asked you for a sample of your writing, you spelt it correctly.'

'If you say so.'

'I do. So when did you discover the proper spelling? Or, more importantly, how did you discover it?'

'I've told you I can't remember.'

'Let me try and help you. You appeared in front of Judge Kilby on Thursday, twenty-second May. The anonymous letter was posted in SE7 on the following Monday and received the next day. It was on Wednesday evening that I met you for the first time in the presence of the head of your Chambers. So it must have been some time between Monday and Wednesday that you found out you had misspelt the judge's name. Am I correct?'

'That lengthy preamble presupposes it was my client who sent the letter,' Rosa broke in quickly.

'It does, indeed, Miss Epton.'

'But my client has not admitted writing the letter.'

'Nor, unless I'm mistaken, has he denied it,' Chantry remarked with a faint sneer.

'May I suggest you move on to another topic?' Rosa said, coldly.

'I'll try and find one on which your client will be more forthcoming.'

There followed a series of questions relating to Duxbury's movements over the weekend.

'May I take it you'd have no objection to my examining this cottage near Guildford?'

Duxbury shot Rosa a quick glance.

'I'm sure that can be arranged,' she said.

'Good. After leaving the pub on Saturday evening, did you by any chance drive up to London?'

'No.'

'It's not very far.'

'I still didn't.'

'I can't help being puzzled by this sudden change in your weekend plans.'

'I've told you. I was feeling depressed and just wanted to get away on my own.'

'Is there anyone who can confirm where you were between, say, eleven o'clock on Saturday night and the early hours of Sunday morning?'

'I was in bed.'

'Yes, but who can confirm it?'

'I don't suppose there's anybody, though I'm sure I'd be remembered at the pub.'

'But you left there by ten-thirty.'

'About then.'

And so the questions ranged back and forth with an alert Rosa ever ready to intervene. She felt the interview had gone as well as could be expected and she wondered what Chantry's next move would be. She certainly wasn't prepared for what came.

She and Peter Duxbury had been left alone in the room while Chantry and Kirkbride withdrew to confer. Rosa thought it likely that Chantry would also be taking advice from his superiors at the Yard.

It was nearly half an hour before Sergeant Kirkbride re-appeared and said that his chief inspector would like to have a word with Rosa. 'He's in the room at the far end of the corridor,' he said, sitting down in the chair Rosa had vacated.

She found Chantry waiting alone. He was standing and came to the point immediately.

'Your client is going to be charged with sending a letter threatening to murder. I've arranged for him to appear before a special court at two o'clock when I shall ask for a remand. I thought you'd like to have advance notice of what's going to happen, Miss Epton.'

'I assume you won't be objecting to bail?' Rosa said in a brittle tone.

'I shall be seeking a remand in custody,' he said with a curtness that seemed to mask a measure of embarrassment.

Rosa had been taken completely by surprise and felt outraged by the abruptness of the decision. Clearly the pressures were on the investigating officer. If she could increase them, so be it. She was now firmly committed to the defence of her, albeit unwelcome, client.

CHAPTER 17

If Rosa had been shaken by the speed of events, Peter Duxbury had been devastated. His mood alternated between violent denunciation of the police and spells of total withdrawal.

She couldn't help reflecting that though most people paid willing lip service to the concept that everybody was equal before the law, they seldom included themselves. Duxbury was furiously indignant at his predicament and muttered dark threats about getting even.

After he had been charged, Rosa phoned Robin and told him what had happened, adding that she hoped to be back in the office by mid-afternoon.

'If the justices refuse bail, will you apply to a judge in Chambers?' Robin asked.

'I can see myself knocking on one judicial door after another,' Rosa said in a resigned tone.

When she arrived at court shortly before two o'clock, the building appeared to be deserted. She was wondering in which of the two court-rooms the hearing was likely to take place when a voice spoke behind her.

'You 'ere for the special?'

She turned to find an usher addressing her from a doorway.

'Yes. Which court shall we be in?'

'Number two. Tuesdays are not one of our regular days. Don't know why it couldn't 'ave waited till tomorrow. What's so special about a barrister? You're not one, are you?' he enquired as an afterthought. Rosa shook her head and he went on, 'Just hope it won't last long. I was reckoning on getting my tomatoes planted out this afternoon.'

'You'll probably manage,' Rosa said in a tone to discourage further confidences.

At that moment a young man came bursting through the main door looking frantically about him. Seeing Rosa and the usher, he stopped in his tracks.

'It hasn't started yet? The special hearing, I mean.'

'No, you've time to get your breath back,' Rosa said.

'I'm press. I was only told fifteen minutes ago and had to drop everything to get here. Are you involved? Can you tell me what it's all about? All I know is that it's something to do with that judge who was murdered over the weekend. They've got the chap, have they?'

'Somebody's been charged with sending her a threatening letter,' Rosa said, turning away.

'But the police think he also killed her, is that the picture?' he asked eagerly.

'You'll have to ask them that.'

'Are you a relative or something?'

'I'm a solicitor.'

'What, the defendant's? That's great, you can give me the low-down.'

Rosa decided he must be as innocent as he was young, his mind bubbling with thoughts of scoops and exclusives.

'There's no low-down,' she said. 'Moreover there'll be very few details you can report.'

'Surely reporting restrictions will be lifted in a case like this?'

'Only on my application and there's no question of that.'

He looked at her like a spaniel suddenly deprived of its walk.

'Couldn't you? I mean, surely the public has a right to know in such an important matter.'

Rosa gave him a withering glance. 'Looking after my client's interests is a good deal more important than satisfying your readers' ghoulish tastes.'

'That's a bit unfair,' he expostulated. 'Newspapers are the bastions of freedom in a democracy.'

He was not only innocent, but starry-eyed as well, she decided. If she didn't get into court soon, he'd start proclaiming the lofty ideals of newspaper proprietors.

She was about to turn away when a familiar figure came through the main door. Frank Petro was a senior member of the crown prosecution service.

'Hello, Rosa,' he called out. 'This shouldn't take long, should it?'

'No time at all if the police don't object to bail.'

'Ah! Like that is it?'

'What'd you expect?'

'I was on my way to another court when I was diverted here, so I've not had time to assess any expectations,' he remarked with a grin. 'I suppose I'd better go and find Chief Inspector Chantry.'

It was a further twenty minutes before everyone had assembled and the hearing could begin. Peter Duxbury sat in the small, railed-off dock with the expression of a sullen child waiting to throw a tantrum.

The clerk asked him to confirm his name and address and then read out the charge.

Frank Petro stood up and said he represented the police and was there to help the court in any way he could. He added that he understood Chief Inspector Chantry was asking for a remand in custody. At this point Chantry went into the witness box and gave short evidence of Peter Duxbury's arrest.

'I'm asking for a remand in custody, Your Worships,' he said.

'Perhaps you'd better tell the court why you oppose bail,' Petro interrupted in a tone of sweet reason.

'Because of the seriousness of the charge and the fact that the recipient of the threatening letter was a judge who has since met a violent death. The police still have many enquiries to make and further charges may follow.'

Rosa knew the standard police reasons for opposing bail as well as she had once known her catechism as a parson's daughter.

The clerk now looked in her direction and she rose to her feet.

'The defendant is a member of the Bar, is he not?' she asked.

'Yes.'

'And has a fixed address?'

'Yes.'

'Also a permanent place in a set of Chambers in the Temple?'

'Yes.'

'So you don't seriously fear that he might abscond, if granted bail?'

'I can't answer that.'

'Why not?'

'Because I can't see into his mind.'

'Would you be prepared to agree to bail if he surrendered his passport and reported daily to the police?'

'I'm still applying for a remand in custody,' Chantry said stonily.

'As to the seriousness of the charge, is it in your view aggravated by Judge Kilby's subsequent death?'

'Naturally.'

'Have you any evidence at all that links the sender of the letter with the murder?'

'As I've already said, there are many further enquiries to be made.'

'Is the answer to my question, no?'

'Our enquiries are still at a preliminary stage.'

Chantry was perfectly used to parrying lawyers' questions and was determined not to concede anything. He needed Peter Duxbury out of the way while he pursued his investigation.

Rosa indicated that she had no further questions to ask (she could recognise a reinforced concrete wall when she met one) and turned to address the two magistrates who had been listening impassively to an oft-enacted scene in their court.

'This case, Your Worships,' Rosa began, 'has more unusual features than a rainbow has colours. A barrister stands charged with sending a letter threatening to murder a judge, who is subsequently killed. Does anyone doubt that bail would have been unopposed had the recipient of the letter still been alive? Difficult though it may be, I ask you to banish from your minds the fact of Judge Kilby's death. It can only prejudice a proper consideration of my client's plea for bail. He has been suddenly enveloped in a nightmare situation and I ask you to end at least part of his present ordeal and give him his liberty.

'He can offer any sureties the police may require and he is willing to abide by such restrictions as the court sees fit to impose. I refer to the surrender of his passport and reporting daily at a police station. It will be many months before this matter reaches trial and it's unthinkable that he should be kept in custody in respect of an offence that seldom incurs a particularly severe penalty.'

'I believe the maximum penalty is ten years' imprisonment,' the clerk broke in, having just looked it up.

'That's correct, though it's also worthwhile noting that the offence was created in eighteen sixty-one, when crime was viewed somewhat differently from today. I invite Your Worships to grant my client bail without any fears of his absconding or interfering with police enquiries. I have nothing further to add.'

The two magistrates picked up their notes and departed through a door at the back of the bench.

Rosa got up and went to speak to Peter Duxbury, who was

sitting glowering at everything in sight.

'The whole thing's a scandal,' he said through clenched teeth. 'It's obvious that Chantry has the court in his pocket and they'll do his bidding. Call it justice!'

'If bail is refused, we'll talk about an application to the judge in Chambers,' Rosa replied, thankful that he was at least partially resigned to the possible loss of his freedom.

He nodded dourly, but said nothing. It was with relief that Rosa saw the magistrates return to court. The chairman adjusted his spectacles and gave a small, authoritative cough.

'The defendant will be remanded in custody for seven days,' he announced. 'We should like to add, however, that the court will reconsider the question of bail at the next hearing.'

Rosa turned in time to quell an apparent outburst from her client.

'That was nicely timed, that look of yours,' Frank Petro remarked as he and Rosa gathered up their papers. 'He could easily have wrecked his chances of bail next time.'

'I'm sure the court doesn't let itself be swayed by spontaneous eruptions on the part of defendants. Even Judge Kilby didn't go that far.'

Petro looked at her with one mildly raised eyebrow. 'Not even if they reveal a violent disposition? A murderer's disposition, for example?'

CHAPTER 18

Tony Kilby (only his mother ever addressed him as Anthony) had spent the past forty-eight hours wondering what to do. He knew that sooner or later the police would track him down and that it might therefore be better to get in touch with them first. The alternative was to fade quietly away. He could always return to Australia where he would have no difficulty in going to ground.

He knew, however, that the police were bound to visit his mother's solicitors and old Percy Bleck would be sure to tell them of his, Tony's, presence in the UK.

He had spoken to his mother on the phone since he came back, but last Saturday was the first time they had met in nearly fifteen years, during which time he had gone from adolescence to adult manhood.

They had dined at a Greek restaurant in Kensington which he suspected she had chosen for its dark atmosphere. A waiter had lit a candle on their table, but she had promptly told him to remove it. She obviously had no wish to be recognised – certainly not in her son's company.

He had accepted her invitation to dinner largely out of curiosity, and had been on his best behaviour in the hope that the evening might bring him good news. It hadn't and he was still wondering why she had wanted to see him. He had referred to his indigent circumstances without receiving any offer of help.

He had got the impression that her own life had reached some sort of turning-point, each of them then unaware how true that was.

He hadn't expected it to be a comfortable evening, which it wasn't. She had questioned him about his plans for the future and he had been evasive, which had irritated her. She liked everyone to have cut and dried plans.

Towards the end of the evening, he asked her about his father, who was nothing more than a blank on his birth certificate.

'I think I have the right to know,' he said, when she turned the subject aside.

'It's none of your business,' she said sharply, which caused him to burst out laughing. It was either that or getting up and walking out in anger.

'At least he gave me a sense of humour. I certainly never inherited that from you. But to get back to the point, I can't think of anything that's more my business.'

'He was a ship that passed in the night and I prefer not to be reminded of him. Anyway, he's now dead.'

'How do you know?'

'Because I made enquiries when I was about to become a judge.'

'I see. Were you afraid he might pop out of the woodwork and create a scandal?'

'He couldn't have done that, anyway. But as I've said he's dead. He died in South America ten years ago.'

'It's a huge continent. Where in South America?'

She hesitated. 'Colombia, if it helps you to know.'

'And you still refuse to tell me his name?'

'There's no point in your knowing.'

'He was my father. There's every point in my knowing.'

'Just accept my word that his name would mean nothing to you.'

'But I'd still like to know. Why shouldn't you tell me?'

'Because for me he died before you were ever born and has been dead ever since.'

'So why are we having dinner this evening? I mean, you must have had a reason for asking me.'

The question seemed to surprise her. 'I thought it was time we met again. You're a grown man now. You've been married . . .'

'And divorced.'

'So you wrote and told me in one of your rare letters.'

'Rare it may have been, but it still didn't get a reply.'

Celia Kilby frowned. She had never liked being reproved, whether it was justified or not.

'I've never pretended to be an affectionate mother, but I have taken an interest in you.'

You could have fooled me, he felt like saying, but refrained.

'So that's the long and short of it? You decided it was time to cast an eye over me again?'

'I wanted to see you, yes.'

'No other motive?'

'What other motive could there be?'

'You might have something momentous to tell me. After all, I've been back in England over a month and yet you've only just suggested we meet.'

'I've been particularly busy of late and usually away at weekends.'

'But not this weekend?'

'I don't like being cross-examined, Anthony,' she said coldly.

'Are we going to meet again? I'd quite enjoy a visit to your court.'

'That's out of the question. But you have my phone number and I'd like you to let me know where I can get in touch with you. I don't imagine you'll be staying indefinitely at that place in Earl's Court.'

After a somewhat lengthy silence he said, 'We seem to have exhausted all our conversation, so I'll get along to one of my watering holes before they close.'

'You can first see me to my car.'

He had done so and she had proffered a cool cheek to be kissed before getting in and driving away.

The time had been exactly ten twenty.

Now, forty-eight hours later, as he looked back over the evening, he realised with the same uncomfortable feeling that the next person she met after leaving him must have been her murderer.

So what should he do? Going to the police might lead to prolonged hassle, but not going could result in worse trouble. He decided to toss a coin. Heads he'd go, tails . . .

It came down heads.

CHAPTER 19

When Friday afternoon finally came, Rosa decided that it had been one of the most exhausting weeks of her life. A disproportionate amount of her time had been spent on Peter Duxbury's case, though, at the end of it all, he was still in custody.

The judge in Chambers had been courteous and benign, but had said he wasn't prepared at that early stage to interfere with the justices' decision. He had caused Rosa to reflect how much more approachable a judge was in his day clothes than when robed and wearing a wig.

She had visited her client in Brixton prison and found him so full of angry resentment at his plight that it was useless trying to

91

have any sort of rational discussion.

That same day she had driven down to the cottage near Albury. It was apparent that the police had been there before her and she could only hope that their visit had been as unproductive as her own. There was no evidence of it having been a murderer's hideout. She found a number of sharp knives in the kitchen, but of a different make from that which had killed Judge Kilby.

It was with a hefty sigh of relief that she left the office on Friday evening and drove home. Peter Chen was coming to dinner the next day and she found herself looking forward to seeing him again after a week's interval.

She rarely entertained at home as her flat was really too small, but occasionally she would invite a friend at the weekend and spend the day preparing everything.

She had decided that, after all the exotic meals she'd had in his company, she would serve him proper English food. The main course would be roast leg of lamb with all the correct trimmings. In view of the warm weather, she thought that jellied consommé, well laced with sherry, would be a pleasant starter and for dessert she proposed to make a raspberry mousse with raspberries Robin had brought her from his garden. She didn't consider herself particularly knowledgeable about wine and always played safe. A Chablis for white and Mouton Cadet for red, with a dry Hock for anyone who wanted to drink wine as an apéritif.

On Saturday morning she got up early, dismissed all thoughts of work from her mind, other than housework, and, armed with a list, went out to buy what she needed for the evening. Thereafter she seemed to spend most of the day in the kitchen. She enjoyed cooking, but couldn't generally be bothered to spend a lot of time preparing meals for herself.

In the afternoon she spent a luxurious hour reading one of the novels forecast to be short-listed for the Booker prize which a friend had recommended. Normally, her leisure reading consisted of twenty minutes in bed at night before she fell asleep.

At six o'clock she had a shower and changed into a crisp linen

92

dress of apple green with a lilac sash.

At half-past seven the doorbell rang and Peter Chen stood on the threshold holding an enormous bouquet of summer flowers.

'Oh, Peter, they're lovely,' Rosa exclaimed after he had kissed her. 'I hope I can find enough vases.'

'Harrods really ought to supply vases with them. Shall I take them back and complain?'

'I've got a better idea. Come in and have a drink.' When they were seated, Rosa with a glass of Chambéry and Peter with a Scotch and water, she said, 'I hope you've had a better week than I have.'

'Possibly more profitable, but almost certainly less interesting. I want to hear all about l'affaire Kilby.'

Rosa retailed the week's events, interrupted only by her dives into the kitchen to switch something on or off.

'Do you believe Duxbury may have murdered her?' Peter asked when she had finished.

She shook her head. 'No, I don't.'

'Is that wishful thinking?'

'Absolutely not. I find him such an unsympathetic person that representing him evokes none of my protective instincts.'

'But you'll continue to stand by him?'

'I haven't any choice. He's relying on me in a way I find embarrassing. I assure you, however, he's a long way from being my favourite client. The trouble is that the police are taking the soft option. They think they can prove he wrote the letter – and, of course, he did – and it follows he must have committed the murder.'

'That means they'll try and make the facts fit a preconceived view and disregard those that don't. They're adept at brushing under the carpet anything that doesn't support their cherished theories. Anyway, what's your next step?'

'I've got to try and find out all I can about Judge Kilby. She wasn't exactly an endearing person and there must be others with stronger motives than Duxbury.'

'How are you going to set about that?'

'There's a barrister called Giles Crowhurst whom I've arranged to meet tomorrow evening at his flat. He's in her old

Chambers and has apparently known her for years. He was also a member of her bridge four and used to see her once a week when they played. The rumour is that he was in love with her.'

'How did you discover all this?'

'Duxbury told me. It seems that, as well as sending her the letter, he did his own research into her habits and background.'

'I don't care for the sound of that.'

'I know. If the police ever found out, it would confirm all their suspicions.'

'And you've already been in touch with Crowhurst?'

Rosa nodded. 'I phoned him yesterday. I thought he might demur at the thought of seeing me. Mind you, he didn't leap at the prospect, but he invited me to his flat for a drink tomorrow evening.'

'What'll be your approach?'

'I shall tell him I don't believe my client killed her, though the police seem intent to pin it on him, and I shall ask him if he has any ideas on the subject.'

'Of course, he may think it was Duxbury.'

'Then I'll have to set off in a different direction.' She jumped up. 'Let's go and eat before everything's burnt or melted.'

He followed her out to the small dining alcove at one end of the kitchen.

'Smells delicious,' he said, sniffing the air like a hungry retriever.

In the event, everything came out as planned and he paid her the ultimate compliment of leaving a clean plate after each course.

After finishing his second helping of mousse, he sat back with a sigh.

'I'll make some coffee,' Rosa said.

While she was doing so, he suddenly came up behind her and gave her neck a quick nuzzle.

'I hope that's not against the house rules?' he said.

'There aren't any house rules.'

'Good,' he said, doing it again.

It was some time later after the coffee things had been

94

removed that he said, 'Would you mind if I stretched out on the sofa?'

'Be my guest!"

'What I hoped you'd say. I can rest my head in your lap and then you won't have to move.'

'I'm no good at massaging scalps if that's what you have in mind.'

'Tell you what, you lie with your head in my lap. I'm very good at scalp massage.'

'But I thought you wanted to stretch out?'

'Perhaps later,' he said, giving her a solemn wink.

Rosa lay with eyes closed while his soothing fingers seemed to draw a whole week's tension out of her body. She wished he'd go on for ever. But then he lowered his head and kissed her on the lips, at first with a sensuously light touch, but soon with quickening desire.

Sunday was the only day of the week that Rosa would even consider taking her car into the City of London. On Sundays the City was a traffic-free oasis compared with other days. On Sundays you could actually park a car, and, by six-thirty in the evening when Rosa arrived in the vicinity of Giles Crowhurst's flat, the last of the tourists had withdrawn to the fleshpots of the West End.

Crowhurst lived on the fifth floor of a block that had been built just after World War II. Now, nearly forty years later, it showed its age and had a run-down appearance. Its hard core of old-time residents, of whom he was one, grumbled about the shabbiness, but, most of all, about the ever-increasing rents. The fact was, however, that it was conveniently located and was an attractive *pied à terre* for those who didn't wish to commute every day. For its permanent residents, it had fewer attractions.

Giles Crowhurst's flat consisted of a single room, with a kitchen the size of a broom cupboard and a bathroom not much larger than the bath itself.

'Miss Epton? Come in, won't you?' he said, opening his front door so abruptly that Rosa was startled. 'It's not very tidy, but then it never is. Convenient, yes; tidy, no.'

It seemed to Rosa as she stepped into the room that every surface was covered with books and magazines – and dust. There was a settee that clearly became a bed at night and he removed a pile of journals from one end.

'Sit there, Miss Epton,' he said, brushing away some crumbs. 'Now, before we begin talking, let me get you a drink. What would you like?'

'Sherry?' Rosa said tentatively.

'Of course. Medium or dry? I'm afraid I don't have the very sweet.'

'Dry, please.'

'I'll join you in that.'

He went over to the curtained-off kitchen and partially disappeared inside.

He looked older than his years, which Rosa knew to be the mid-forties. He had a kind face, but his eyes gave him a defeated look. The sort of look that proclaimed someone who was used to failure.

He handed her a glass of sherry and sat down on a chair set against the opposite wall, where a table served every purpose from writing desk to dining surface.

'So you're representing Duxbury,' he said, giving Rosa a thoughtful look.

'Yes. Do you know him?'

He shook his head. 'Never come across him, but then my practice doesn't take me into criminal courts.'

From all Rosa had heard, it took him into very few courts.

'I understand you were a long-time friend of Judge Kilby's?' she said.

'I knew her for more than twenty years. I joined our Chambers a few years after she did and we shared a room right up to the time she became a judge.'

'Then you obviously knew her very well.'

He nodded. 'Yes, I suppose I did.' After a pause he went on, 'I think, Miss Epton, it would be best if you put your cards on the table. What exactly is it you hope to find out from me?'

'That's a fair question,' Rosa said with a smile. 'It's clear that the police are hoping to pin Judge Kilby's murder on my client. He professes complete innocence. In those circumstances it behoves me to probe around a bit.'

'And you think I can help you in that respect?'

'Can you?'

'Let me first ask you this, does your client also deny sending the letter threatening to murder?'

'He's made no admissions to the police,' Rosa said carefully.

'Not to the police, eh! Anyway, that's really none of my business. Where do you want to begin?'

Rosa took a deep breath. 'As you probably know, Judge Kilby had the reputation of being difficult in court . . .'

'It's all right, Miss Epton, you needn't beat about the bush. From all accounts, she could be a pig to all and sundry when she was sitting. I may add that she was well aware of her reputation, but she'd never been a person to take soft options or curry favour and she didn't care whose toes she trod on once she felt her duty demanded a certain course of action.' He gave a deep sigh. 'She was a very remarkable woman with many fine qualities, though I'm afraid humility was not one of them. She could be kind and generous to her friends, but she seemed to lack any streak of compassion in her make-up.' Rosa watched with alarm as he put up a hand to brush away a tear. 'I was very, very fond of her, but that didn't blind me to her faults.' He gave Rosa a misty look. 'It's not really a secret any longer that I'd have liked to marry her.'

'Her death must have come as a terrible shock to you.'

'Yes, a terrible shock. I still find it difficult to comprehend. There's nothing quite as final as sudden death.'

'Feeling about her as you did, you must have given a lot of thought as to who could have killed her?'

He seemed to sink into a reverie and Rosa was unsure whether he was going to answer. But after a pause during which a nearby church clock struck seven, he spoke again.

'She was somebody who tended to keep her relationships in separate compartments,' he said slowly. 'With Celia it was never a case of your friends are my friends, and she kept certain aspects of her life very much to herself.' He gave Rosa a look of

97

appraisal as if trying to decide how much to say. 'For example, I discovered only a few years ago that she had an illegitimate son. She had never mentioned it all the time we'd known each other. It showed how secretive she could be.'

'How did you find out?' Rosa asked with interest.

He grimaced. 'I was at her flat for bridge one evening and happened to go into her study. There was a letter from an Anthony Kilby in Australia on her desk. She came in while I was there and was absolutely furious. She accused me of spying on her, when all I was doing was looking for a sheet of paper.'

'Nevertheless, she told you that Anthony Kilby was her son?'

'It didn't come out as simply as that. I was stung by her reaction and we had quite a row, in the course of which she told me more out of defiance than anything else that yes, he was her son, that he had been born to her when she was nineteen and had just started studying for the Bar and now was my curiosity satisfied?' He paused and finished his sherry. 'It was the only real row we ever had.'

Rosa imagined there could have been many more had Giles Crowhurst not been such a complaisant person.

He sprang up from his chair. 'Let me refill your glass, Miss Epton.'

When he had done so and sat down again, he went on, 'I mention that only as evidence of an almost obsessive secretiveness. But to get back to your original question as to who might have killed her – and assuming for the moment that it wasn't your client – I can offer you two possible lines of enquiry. Celia was in a permanent state of war with her landlord, who wanted vacant possession of the house, but she always managed to thwart his plans. He's a singularly nasty individual to whom dirty tricks would come naturally.'

'There's a big difference between dirty tricks and murder,' Rosa broke in.

'The difference between marijuana and heroin. The one often leads on to the other. Bernard Riscock is a ruthless property developer who's used to getting his own way. I'm not suggesting he killed her with his own hands, but I'm sure he keeps hired thugs in a back room. Celia herself certainly believed him capable of violence and with her out of the way the other tenants would be no match for him. Anyway, if you're making a list of suspects, you may like to put Mr Riscock on it.'

'You mentioned a possible second line of enquiry,' Rosa said.

'This may be something or nothing. The fact is that Celia had suddenly taken to going away at weekends. To somewhere near Horsham in Sussex. My guess is that she visited a friend, a man friend, and stayed with him. Not long before her death when she said she was going down to Sussex for the weekend, I mentioned I didn't recall her having friends in that area. She promptly snubbed me and, in effect, told me to mind my own business. This last weekend was the first one she stayed at home, and she was murdered. That could be significant, don't you think?'

'It's easier to think of a hundred innocent explanations than a sinister one,' Rosa observed. 'She may have stayed in London to attend the Gillett Society garden party. I saw her there myself.'

'It would take more than a garden party to keep Celia in London if she had better things to do in the country.'

'What exactly are you suggesting?'

'That you try and find out about her mysterious Sussex weekends. Whom did she visit and why didn't she go last weekend? There may, as you say, be a perfectly innocent answer to the latter question, but I know I'd want to probe that angle if I were you.' He gave her a small twisted smile. 'Even if I was the investigating officer.'

'With no name and no address, where do I start?' Rosa said with a sigh.

'That's where the police may be able to help you. I imagine they've taken possession of her diary and address book, though, knowing Celia, they mayn't be all that informative. She was rather fond of identifying people simply by initial letters.'

'I doubt whether the police are interested in anything that doesn't point to my client's guilt.'

'It's extraordinary to think of a barrister being suspected of murder. And yet even stranger things happen these days.'

'Like judges being murdered!'

'That certainly makes it even more bizarre,' he agreed.

CHAPTER 20

Monday morning found Chantry and Kirkbride back in the Deputy Assistant Commissioner's office.

'You're not going to be able to hold Duxbury in custody beyond his next appearance,' the DAC said, after they had been talking a while.

'I realise that, sir, but I still regard him as the prime suspect,' Chantry said doggedly.

'Maybe you do, but you don't have any evidence. The cottage at Albury didn't produce any and the lab hasn't been able to come up with anything that links him to the scene of the crime. And if forensic can't help you, you're not going to get anywhere. Added to all of which you tell me this morning that the original threatening letter and the note pinned to the deceased's back were written with different pens.'

'That doesn't mean they weren't written by the same person, sir.'

'More to the point, it certainly doesn't prove that they were.' He gave Chantry an uncompromising look. 'You're back at square one, Alan. Maybe we need a fresh mind on the case. You still have *my* confidence, but the ACC thinks we ought to have a chief superintendent in charge of the investigation. It's proving a harder nut to crack than we thought. And, after all, it's not just a murder, but the murder of a judge. The establishment doesn't like that sort of thing, it makes them restive.'

'Does that mean I'm being taken off the case?' Chantry asked bleakly.

'No, but I can't promise you'll be left in charge if we don't get results quickly. I think you must look at things from a fresh angle. Accept that the writer of the threatening letter and the murderer could be different people. There must be others with a motive for killing our unpopular lady judge.'

'Sergeant Kirkbride has spent two days going through court records looking for clues, sir.'

The DAC gave an impatient shake of his head. 'You're going to find the murderer much closer to home than that. I've never believed for a moment that the Pashley family was involved. It's not their sort of crime.'

'I agree, sir. Much more likely to have been Duxbury. He felt Judge Kilby had put paid to his career and he was heard to utter threats against her. Moreover we know he has a violent temper.'

'Forget Duxbury for a moment,' the DAC said with a sigh. 'What about the son, Anthony Kilby? That's an extraordinary story. He comes back from Australia after twelve years and then has dinner with his mother the very night she's murdered.'

'He'd hardly have come forward, sir, if he was the murderer.'

'He might have a motive for doing just that. It wouldn't be the first time a murderer has offered his co-operation to the police. Before being caught, I mean. I think we need to take a much closer look at him.'

'He does have an alibi, sir.'

The DAC snorted. 'You can get yourself an alibi in Earl's Court as easily a take-away dinner.' He glanced down at the file in front of him. 'And what about this man, Riscock? He sounds a right villain. Has a record for violence, too, I see.'

'That was twenty years ago, sir, when he was a young man. He also has an alibi.'

'His type has alibis for every day of the week. The young thug turned unscrupulous entrepreneur. If Judge Kilby stood between him and half a million pounds, I doubt whether he'd have any qualms about arranging her swift transition from this life to the next.' He glanced at Kirkbride who was wriggling on his chair. 'Yes, William, do you want to go to the loo or make a contribution to what's being said?'

'The latter, sir. There's frequent reference in Judge Kilby's diary to somebody who is only identified as E. She appears to have spent almost every weekend with him . . .'

'Him?'

'I surmise that "E" is a he, sir,' Kirkbride said with a flicker of a smile.

'How do the entries appear in her diary?'

'Saturday and Sunday are bracketed together with 'At E's" written beside the bracket.'

101

'So who is this "E"?' the DAC asked, looking from one to the other. Chantry, however, was plainly leaving the floor to his sergeant.

'I think he could be somebody whose initials are EM,' Kirkbride went on. 'There's an EM with a telephone number at the back of the diary, together with other numbers. The code is that for Horsham. I've been in touch with the police there and they say that the subscriber is an Edward Maxwell. He's a wealthy widower who lives at somewhere called Brake's Farm.'

'Have you been in touch with him yet?'

'No, sir. He apparently went away in the middle of last week. He has a live-in Portuguese couple, who don't know when he'll be back. If E and EM are the same person, there's one rather significant fact. Judge Kilby had spent the last six weekends at E's, but not the weekend she was killed. And yet Mr Maxwell was home that weekend.'

'But has now gone away?'

'Exactly, sir.'

'I think one of you ought to go down today and interview the staff. If Judge Kilby used to stay there, they must know. Let's get the mystery of E cleared up as soon as possible. We don't want any mystery men, or women, cluttering up the enquiry.' He glanced at his watch. 'I've got a meeting in about ten minutes. Anything else either of you want to say before we break up? We'll meet again tomorrow morning. Meanwhile I'll talk to the ACC. Perhaps we should set up further teams to target different aspects.'

'There is one other thing, sir . . .' Chantry began.

'Yes? Quick then.'

'The note that was pinned to the dead woman's back. It didn't have any creases.'

'So?'

'It couldn't have been folded.'

'You mean, the murderer couldn't have carried it in his pocket?'

'Right, sir.'

'I suppose it could have been in a briefcase or bag, together with the murder weapon.'

102

'I think it's more likely he wrote it in Judge Kilby's flat after killing her and then returned to pin it on her body.'

'Could he have got into her flat?'

'Easily. The door key was in her handbag which was lying close to her body. He could have taken it and put it back again.'

'Were there similar sheets of paper in her flat?'

Chantry nodded. 'It could have been taken from a pad we found in her study. The sort you buy at law stationers.'

'Has forensic examined the pad?'

'Yes, sir, but I'm afraid they didn't find any indentation marks indicating he had written the note on the pad itself.'

The DAC sighed. 'The murderer, whoever he was, seems to have gone well prepared. He took a knife with him and must also have worn gloves as he didn't leave any fingerprints. He either knew the time of Judge Kilby's return or, at least, was prepared to wait for her.' He shot Chantry a thoughtful look. 'Who knew better the hour of her return than her son?'

'According to him, he saw her to her car and watched her drive off. She'd have been home before he could have got there.'

'Only two people knew whether that's true and one of them is dead,' the DAC remarked. 'If you're right about the note having been written in her flat, it means the murderer hung about the scene for much longer than necessary. He was running the helluva risk.'

'Not really, sir. The path that leads from the garages to the house is secluded and he wasn't likely to be seen or heard.'

'Nevertheless ...' The phone on the DAC's desk gave a furious buzz and he lifted the receiver. 'Yes, I'm coming right away,' he said, springing from his chair and making a dash for the door. 'Call me this afternoon. Meanwhile you must keep up the momentum. An enquiry that loses its momentum soon becomes a lost cause.' He vanished, leaving behind only the smell of pipe smoke.

'The DAC's a bit like a conjuror trying to keep half a dozen coloured balls up in the air at the same time,' Chantry observed. 'Ours is the red one.'

'Well, I might as well take off for Horsham, sir,' Kirkbride

103

said, standing up and stretching himself. 'I take it, you don't want to come, too?'

'It's the last thing I want to do. It'll be a waste of time. There are more important things to do at this end.'

Sergeant Kirkbride felt pretty sure that the so-called more important things related to the DCI's continuing determination to focus his attention on Duxbury. It was plain that nothing the DAC had said had convinced him that his investigation was off course. Kirkbride, who liked and respected both the DAC and Alan Chantry, prayed that the enquiry wouldn't turn into a personal crusade, for that wouldn't do anybody good.

As Chantry and Kirkbride arrived back at the station where they had established their headquarters, one of the young detective constables on the investigating team held out the telephone to Chantry.

'It's Mrs Spicer, sir. She's asked for you by name.'

Chantry waved the instrument away. 'You speak to her, Bill. Tell her I'm out.'

Kirkbride took the receiver. 'Detective Sergeant Kirkbride here, can I help you?'

'It's Mrs Spicer. I wished to speak to the chief inspector.'

'I'm afraid he's not available. If it's information you have, perhaps you'd tell me.'

Adèle Spicer took an audible breath. 'One of your young men came to see me last week after I'd got in touch with the police. You see, I was a close friend of Judge Kilby's and used to see her at least once a week when we met for bridge.' The DC waved the short statement she had made in front of Kirkbride. He remembered having read it. Indeed, Giles Crowhurst and Norman Ackroyd, whom she had mentioned as fellow bridge players, had also been interviewed, though it appeared that neither had any useful information to give. Mrs Spicer was, meanwhile, gushing on. 'You see, at the time I gave my statement, I understood that young barrister was about to be charged with her murder, but, from what I've since read in the papers, I gather you're still in the dark as to who committed such a terrible crime. That's why I'm phoning you now; you see, I may have information that could help you.'

104

'What's the nature of your information, Mrs Spicer?' Kirkbride broke in, hoping to stem the flow of words and bring her to the point.

'If you'll give me time, I was just coming to that. Celia, that is Judge Kilby, had recently been going down to Sussex for weekends. Somewhere near Horsham. She was somewhat mysterious about her visits and brushed aside questions she didn't wish to answer. And that seemed to upset Mr Crowhurst. He was one of our bridge four and had known Celia a great many years. Even so, she used to be quite offhand with him at times, not that he ever seemed to bear her any grudge, though there was an occasion at her flat a few weeks ago when his usually benign mood seemed to have deserted him . . .'

'Are you suggesting that Mr Crowhurst might have had a motive for the murder?'

There was a moment's stunned silence before Mrs Spicer exclaimed in a tone of some alarm, 'Oh, good gracious, no! I never meant anything of the sort. It's a ridiculous idea. Giles is a charming man and he'd have been the last person to wish Celia any harm.'

Kirkbride sighed. 'You were mentioning her weekend visits to Horsham. . .'

'Yes, that's what I was about to tell you when you sidetracked me.' She paused. 'May I be assured that you will treat anything I say in confidence?'

'You may be assured of that.'

Mrs Spicer lowered her voice and went on, 'I have no doubt in my own mind that Celia had found herself a lover. My female instinct tells me so and it's never wrong.'

'Have you any idea as to his identity?'

'No. As I've said, Celia was most secretive about her weekends, but a woman can tell when one of her friends is having an affair.'

'Not all affairs end up in murder.'

'As a policeman, you should be aware how many do,' she remarked severely. 'Anyway, if you're looking for Celia's murderer, I think you should follow up the information I've given you.'

'Thank you for your help, Mrs Spicer. I've noted what you've said.'

He had no intention of telling her that he'd been about to set out for Horsham when she called. But she had succeeded in confirming the need for his visit.

The most significant fact was Edward Maxwell's failure, eight days after the murder, to have come forward. Indeed, to have left home and gone away.

Maria da Costa was washing the paintwork of Mr Maxwell's bedroom at Brake's Farm when she heard a car pull up outside. She thought it must be her husband back sooner than expected from an expedition into Horsham to buy a fitting for the bathroom of their own quarters over the stables, which were located some seventy yards from the house itself. For Maria, having a bathroom with running hot and cold water had been the greatest luxury in their move to England. She and Luiz came from a poor mountain village in eastern Portugal where such luxuries were unknown.

There had been times during the past year, however, when she had wondered whether the joy of running water within her home was adequate compensation for all the rain that poured down outside. English summer weather with its overcast skies, chilly winds and frequent rain was, she felt, something that had to be experienced to be believed.

She dropped her cloth back into the bucket and went across to the window in time to see a strange man getting out of a strange car. He glanced up at the house and spotted her before she had time to move away. Committed, now, to answering the door she went downstairs and pulled back two heavy bolts before unlocking it. She always shut herself in firmly when she was alone in the house.

'Mrs da Costa?' the man enquired. She nodded cautiously. 'I'm Detective Sergeant Kirkbride of the Metropolitan Police.' She quickly crossed herself. 'I'd like to have a word with you. May I come in?'

Watching him as though he were a cobra who might strike without warning, she stood aside to let him enter.

'Do you understand English?'

'A leetle.' In fact she understood it rather better than she

106

spoke it, but felt safer not admitting the fact.

'I understand Mr Maxwell is away?' She nodded warily. 'Can you tell me when he'll be back?'

She shook her head and uttered a harsh 'no'.

'Did he not tell you when to expect his return?'

'No.'

'Where has he gone?'

'He away.'

'I know. But where?'

'Not say.'

'Did he take much luggage with him?'

She looked puzzled and Kirkbride produced a piece of mime, which, rather to his surprise, she seemed to understand.

'One luggage,' she said. Then added, 'One luggage and one baggage.'

Further mime elucidated that she meant a suitcase and a travel bag.

'Did he take his passport?' She shrugged. 'So you don't know whether he's gone abroad?' Another shrug. 'Have you heard of Judge Kilby?'

'Judge?'

'Kilby. She used to spend weekends here with Mr Maxwell, yes?'

'Mr Maxwell's friend come. I not know her name.'

'Did you meet her?' Kirkbride asked, producing a somewhat incongruous photograph of the judge in full judicial regalia.

'No,' she said in her harsh voice.

'Never?'

'No.'

'But surely you must have caught sight of her when she was here?'

'No, Mr Maxwell live here. We live there.' She gestured in the direction of the stables and Kirkbride noticed her hands for the first time. They were hands which had known a lifetime of manual labour, rough and striated.

'Do you read English newspapers?' She shook her head as though he had insulted her. Perhaps he had.

'I'm sure you watch television?'

107

'My husband watch football.'

'And you?'

'I watch only quiz show.'

Kirkbride sighed. 'Did you know that Judge Kilby was dead? That she'd been murdered?'

Her hands flew up to her face before she hurriedly crossed herself again.

'I do not know,' she said, in a tone both obstinate and alarmed.

Kirkbride realised he had reached the end of his immediate mission. He was now satisfied that the person identified as 'E' in Judge Kilby's diary was indeed Edward Maxwell. Whether Mrs da Costa could tell him any more if she were willing was problematic. It seemed unlikely that she had been ignorant of a murder that had been widely reported over the past week, not only in the newspapers but also on television.

Perhaps it was loyalty to her employer, allied to fear of the police in a foreign country, that had prevented her saying more. Even so, he doubted whether she had any further useful information to give. It wasn't as if Judge Kilby had met her end at Brake's Farm and it was fanciful to imagine that Edward Maxwell would have confided in his Portuguese staff.

He was therefore reasonably satisfied with what he had achieved. There might not be any evidence to justify a manhunt for the missing Mr Maxwell, but steps would need to be taken to interview him as soon as he reappeared.

CHAPTER 21

Two days later Rosa returned to the magistrates' court to renew her application for bail on Peter Duxbury's remand appearance.

She arrived early in order to visit him in the cells beforehand. Barely had she entered his presence before he launched into a diatribe about his treatment in prison and the scandalous way the police had behaved. He expressed his determination to sue for false imprisonment and malicious prosecution. His career might have been wrecked, but let nobody think his spirit was broken.

Rosa listened to him in patient silence. It would have been fruitless to remind him that he had admitted the offence with which he stood charged. He spoke as if he had already been indicted for murder.

'The whole legal system is archaic and weighted in favour of the police,' he said bitterly.

Rosa reflected that circumstances certainly altered cases. She doubted whether he would have uttered the same condemnation a few weeks ago when he'd been a complacent, self-satisfied young member of his profession. Not only had his views undergone a startling transformation, but he had changed physically as well. His eyes would suddenly light up with piercing fanaticism and he had developed a slight twitch down the right side of his face. It was an alarming deterioration in a single week and it filled Rosa with foreboding.

'Where will you stay, if the court grants bail?' she asked.

'At home, of course.'

'Mightn't it be better to get away from London for a while?'

'I've got a perfectly good flat and I shall go there,' he said brusquely. 'If I find that the police have tampered with any of my possessions, I'll sue.'

Rosa decided to let the matter rest. She gave him an encouraging smile and went upstairs to court.

"Morning, Rosa,' Frank Petro greeted her.

'I wondered if you'd be here again,' she remarked. 'Presumably Chief Inspector Chantry still feels in need of moral support.'

'I'm just here to see fair play,' he said lightly.

'Are the police still opposing bail?'

'I gather so.'

'On what grounds?'

'The same as last week.'

'Between ourselves is Chantry any nearer preferring a charge of murder against my client?'

'Between ourselves, no.'

'Or against anyone else?'

'Same answer.'

'Do you know anything about a mysterious man friend Judge Kilby had?'

'Are you referring to somebody who lives in the Horsham area?' Rosa nodded, and he went on, 'I believe they have tried to interview such a person, but that he has gone away.'

'Could you tell me his name?'

'Edward Maxwell. Now, stop pumping me or I may say something indiscreet.'

Rosa grinned. 'Thanks, Frank. As always you've been most helpful.'

A minute or two later, the clerk came bustling in. Addressing the two lawyers, he said, 'I'll call your case on first and then you can get away.'

On this occasion not only was the press bench packed, but it seemed there wasn't an empty space in the whole court. Admittedly it was one of their regular sitting days, but Rosa surmised it was round two in the case of R. *v.* Duxbury that was the main attraction. With reporting restrictions unlifted, however, the press was in for a frustrating time.

As soon as the three magistrates had taken their places, Peter Duxbury was brought into the dock and Chief Inspector Chantry walked briskly to the witness box.

Rosa glanced at her client, who was wearing an expression of sullen martyrdom.

Frank Petro rose to his feet with an air of a performer waiting for the applause to die down. 'What is the position in this case, Chief Inspector?' he said.

'I'm applying for a further remand in custody, Your Worships,' Chantry intoned. 'We still have many enquiries to make regarding Judge Kilby's death and the threatening letter she received.'

Petro sat down and the clerk peered at Rosa.

'Are you renewing your application for bail, Miss Epton?'

'Yes.'

'Do you wish to ask Chief Inspector Chantry any questions?'

'If it please Your Worships,' Rosa said, turning to face the witness. 'Would I be right in thinking that your opposition to bail is based on your expectation of being able to charge my client with Judge Kilby's murder?'

Chantry shifted his stance as though he'd been suddenly prodded with a sharp spike.

'No,' he said, after what seemed an unduly long pause.

'What is it based on then?'

'The seriousness of the charge preferred against him.'

'And that's the only ground?'

'Yes. It is a serious charge.'

'Would you agree that it's an offence that can vary from, say, the letting off of a bit of steam by somebody suffering from considerable frustration to a determined threat actually to murder the person to whom the letter is sent?'

'The seriousness of any individual offence is for the court to decide,' Chantry said, obviously pleased with his reply.

'But I'm asking you the question as an experienced police officer.'

'Every offence has differing degrees of seriousness,' he said, warily.

'In your experience is this particular offence, more often than not, committed by the frustrated, rather than by potential murderers?'

'I'm afraid I don't have any statistics on the subject.'

'No, but you have a wealth of practical experience; and also, if I may say so, an abundance of common sense.' He shot her a suspicious look which Rosa fielded with a faint smile. 'I know better than to try and win you over by flattery, Mr Chantry; I'm simply calling on your knowledge as a senior police officer.'

'I don't think my knowledge can help you,' he said in a tone that was even invested with a note of regret. 'As a matter of fact,' he added as an apparent afterthought, 'I've only ever dealt with one previous case of sending a letter threatening to murder and that was nearly twenty years ago.'

'What rank were you then?' Rosa enquired mildly.

'I was a detective constable.'

'Nevertheless, you were left to deal with such a serious case on your own?' She cocked her head on one side like a bird anticipating the appearance of a worm. 'May one ask what the result was?'

Chantry threw her a pained look. 'The defendant was put on probation.'

'I have no further questions to ask,' Rosa said and sat down.

'You wish to address their worships?' the clerk said.

Rosa pushed back her hair which had fallen forward on both sides of her face and stood up again.

'Last week the court indicated that it would be prepared to reconsider the question of bail when the defendant came before it today.

'Let me make it clear at the outset that nothing I say is intended as a criticism of Detective Chief Inspector Chantry. He has his job to do and I have mine.

'It's quite apparent, is it not, that police enquiries into Judge Kilby's death are nowhere near a conclusion? We have heard nothing of an imminent arrest or of a quick solution to the case.

'My client had nothing to do with her death, but, having been charged with sending her a letter threatening to murder, he finds himself engulfed by a tidal wave of hideous suspicion. Some unknown person murdered Judge Kilby and thereby ensured that an accusing finger would point at the defendant. It is indeed a nightmare situation for him. The nightmare will remain whatever your decision about bail, but you can at least alleviate it by releasing him from custody.

'As you're aware, he is a member of the Bar with a place in a prestigious set of Chambers and he has a fixed abode, namely a flat of which he's the owner. The last thing he would be likely to do is abscond. He's in sufficient trouble without adding to it by turning himself into a fugitive from justice.

'He's ready to surrender his passport to the police and he can offer such sureties as the court may see fit to order.

'In all those circumstances, I urge Your Worships to grant the defendant bail.'

As the magistrates retired to their room, Frank Petro turned to Rosa.

'It's a walkover,' he said.

'Do you really think so?'

'Of course it is. It'll teach Chantry to keep his reminiscences to himself.'

'He was certainly more helpful than he intended.'

'It's always satisfying to lure a witness into saying a bit too much.'

'I wasn't even trying to catch him out.'

'As you and I both know, justice is a vast lottery.' He glanced towards the bench. 'The soothsayers are coming back.'

Five minutes later Peter Duxbury was standing beside Rosa, looking tense and ill at ease. The magistrates had granted him bail in his own recognisance of £2,000 and with one surety in a like sum. They had also ordered that he should surrender his passport to the police.

The surety was to be his cousin, with whom he had planned to stop the night after his abortive attempt at burgling Snaith and Epton's office. Rosa had been in touch with him during the past week and he had readily agreed to stand bail if the court granted it. She had the impression that he somehow felt guilty over what had happened. If he'd been at home that night, it wouldn't have happened et cetera . . . It wasn't true, of course, and Rosa surmised that something else had given him a guilty conscience.

'Where are you heading for from here?' Rosa asked, as Duxbury stood beside her in a brooding silence.

'Home. To think.'

'I'll drive you.'

'Thanks.'

He was wearing a burglar's outfit which consisted of a pair of jeans, a T-shirt and a red zip-up nylon jacket. In his hand he held a crumpled carrier bag containing the few possessions he'd had with him in prison. He was a far removed figure from the uppity young barrister who had confronted Rosa the first time they met.

The case had been adjourned for six weeks which gave everyone time to consider their positions. The charge of sending a letter threatening to murder could only be dealt with by the crown court which meant that the prosecution would have to present its evidence and ask for a committal for trial at the higher court. As far as Rosa could foresee, the evidence would consist of her client's proved misspelling of Judge Kilby's name, plus the overheard verbal threats he had made after the case, plus, possibly, some sort of forensic evidence.

It remained to be seen whether she could get the magistrates to dismiss the charge on the basis of no case to answer. If this could be done without calling on Duxbury to go into the witness-box, that would be fine. If, however, he intended swearing on oath that he had never sent the letter, he would have to find another lawyer. Rosa fought hard for her clients, but refused to overstep the ethical mark. Skating on thin ice was one thing, professional dishonesty another.

For most of the journey, Duxbury sat in a withdrawn silence, clutching his bag of possessions on his lap as though expecting them to be snatched away. She was relieved when they reached the house in which he had the top-floor flat. Almost immediately a photographer sprang forward from a neighbouring doorway and a reporter thrust a tape recorder through the half-open passenger window. Rosa didn't hesitate, but re-engaged a gear and accelerated away to an angry shout from the reporter whose tape recorder fell to the ground.

Duxbury let out a groan. 'What am I going to do now?'

'Go and stay with your cousin for a few days.'

A stubborn expression came over his face. 'I'm buggered if I'm going to let the press get me on the run. It's my home and if I have any trouble, I'll phone the police. The local police,' he added pointedly. 'I'm having no truck with Chantry until we bury him beneath a shower of writs.'

Rosa held her peace. It wasn't the moment to tell him that he had as much hope of successfully suing the police as a convicted murderer had of getting probation.

'Drop me off here,' he said, indicating a public house they were approaching. 'I need a drink.'

'Keep in touch with me,' Rosa said as he prepared to get out. 'We've got a lot to discuss before we go back to court.'

He nodded grimly. 'I wonder who did murder the bitch? Who do you think did it?'

'It seems to me it must have been someone who knew her. Someone who had a score to settle. That note pinned to her body was written by someone seeking vengeance and not minding that the world should know.'

'I fit that description.'

'I know you've admitted sending her the letter, but I accept

114

that you didn't kill her.'

'Chantry's still certain I did.'

'I know, though I think he may be beginning to have a few niggling doubts.' Rosa was thoughtful for a moment. 'To get Chantry off your back, we need to present him with an alternative target.'

'Who do you have in mind?'

'I'll tell you when I'm more sure of my ground. My worry is that unless Celia Kilby's murderer is found, you're likely to remain under suspicion for the rest of your life. That's where the person who killed her has been so clever. He's exploited your situation to full advantage.'

CHAPTER 22

It was the day after Peter Duxbury's release on bail and Chief Inspector Chantry was feeling deeply frustrated. He realised that the investigation was in danger of losing the vital impetus of which the DAC had spoken. Moreover, it now seemed certain that one of CI's detective chief superintendents would be assigned to the case with a view to directing and co-ordinating enquiries. Admittedly, he, Chantry, wasn't being taken off it, but he'd no longer be his own master.

He'd been so sure Duxbury had committed the murder that he had neglected other lines of enquiry. His was far from being the first investigation to run into the ground, but it didn't do one's career any good. He had also learnt that a question was to be put to the Home Secretary in the House about the conduct of the enquiry.

'Was the Home Secretary satisfied that enquiries into Judge Kilby's death were being pursued with sufficient determination?'

It was all most depressing and Chantry blamed nobody but himself for the failure to make an arrest. An arrest for murder, that is. He felt like a student who, after covering several pages of exam paper, discovers that he has entirely misread the question.

115

As he sat ploughing his way through all the statements for the umpteenth time, hoping that some overlooked clue would suddenly leap out at him, he longed for something to happen to break the impasse.

Appeals had gone out for Edward Maxwell to make himself known to the police who were anxious to interview him, but so far he had not appeared. Efforts to discover his whereabouts were being intensified, though apparently with no success.

Tony Kilby, for his part, was still at his Earl's Court hotel and had promised to let the police know if he moved.

His mother, meanwhile, lay in the mortuary refrigerator awaiting the coroner's order. That functionary hesitated to release the body for cremation (as directed in Judge Kilby's will) until an arrest had been made and he could be certain that the cause of death was not likely to be disputed.

Mr Percy Bleck viewed the delay with the utmost distaste, but was given no say in the matter.

'Please let something happen, please give me a break,' Chantry said out loud to a faded studio photograph of a long deceased Commissioner of Police that hung on the opposite wall.

'Am I interrupting something?' Kirkbride said coming into the room at that moment.

'I was only talking to myself,' Chantry remarked. Then noticing Kirkbride's expression, he added, 'What's happened now?'

'There's been an explosion at Eight Aubusson Way. Nobody's been hurt, but there's been a fair amount of structural damage.'

Chantry frowned while he tried to decide whether this might be the break he'd been praying for or whether it was merely an irrelevant complication.

'When did it happen?'

'About two hours ago.'

'What sort of explosion was it?'

'It appears to have been gas. I gather there was a strong smell of gas in the house two days ago, which Miss Cherry reported. She has the ground-floor flat. Two fitters came round and apparently identified the source of the leak in the basement. They replaced a length of pipe and departed. And then about seven-thirty this morning, there was this explosion. Now the whole place is crawling with Gas Board officials. The suggestion is, of course, that the fitters made a botched job, which resulted in today's explosion.'

'Is that what you think, Bill?'

'I imagine my thoughts are the same as yours, sir. I'd like to get along there as soon as possible and interview everyone within sight.'

'After which we may wish to interview somebody who almost certainly won't be within sight.'

'Bernard Riscock?'

'Exactly.'

The two officers arrived in Aubusson Way to find it so swarming with Gas Board vans as to make it seem they were holding a rally. There were two police cars parked outside number eight and a uniform constable was shepherding people away from the entrance.

As the house came into view up the drive, they could see a number of shattered windows and the main front door looking as though a giant had tried to wrench it off.

'I suggest we speak to Miss Cherry first,' Kirkbride said. 'She was the one who reported the leak and she'll be a better witness than the other two. Mr Gilfroy is in his seventies and extremely deaf and Mrs Ives is a nervous widow who introduces her late husband into everything. I had a terrible time trying to interview her after Judge Kilby's death.'

They found Miss Cherry in her ground-floor flat sweeping up broken glass. She was in her fifties and worked as a physiotherapist at a nearby hospital. She greeted the two officers briskly.

'You don't mind if I go on clearing up, do you, but I'm due at the hospital at one and would like to get the place tidy before I leave.'

'I believe you reported the smell of gas two days ago?' Chantry said.

'Yes, I smelt it when I came in about four o'clock that afternoon. It was quite strong in the entrance hall and I decided

117

it was coming up from the basement where all the meters are housed and where the main gas supply enters the house. I phoned the gas people immediately and a couple of men came round within half an hour.' She gave them a quick sardonic smile. 'If you want prompt attention, just mention a leak. They were here about fifty minutes and I made a point of seeing them before they left. They said a small pipe leading into Mr Gilfroy's meter had a slight crack in it and that they'd replaced it and that all would now be well. Certainly there was no further smell of gas after they'd gone. Yesterday everything seemed all right and then today this happened.'

'Did you smell gas this morning?'

'No. I was still in bed when it occurred.'

'Do you have any theories, Miss Cherry?'

'Theories? That's a funny word to use.' She paused. 'Though I suppose I can guess what you're getting at. Namely, could this have been engineered by our landlord as part of his campaign to get us out? That's what you're really asking, isn't it? You obviously know all about Mr Riscock and his efforts to get vacant possession. Of course, he had no chance while Judge Kilby was alive. She thwarted him at every turn, but now our champion is no longer with us. I, in fact, am giving up my tenancy at the end of the year. I've had the offer of a job in New Zealand where my only brother lives. Mrs Ives and Mr Gilfroy have, until now, been determined to hang on.' She stared thoughtfully at the dustpan in her hand. 'Theories,' she repeated. 'I understand that one of Mr Riscock's men was here the day I smelt the gas. I didn't see him myself, but Mrs Ives said he'd been examining the roof.'

'When would that have been?'

'Some time in the afternoon.'

'So he could also have gone down to the basement?'

'Very easily.'

'Are Mr Riscock's men often here?'

'Quite often. One's never sure what they're up to, but there's nothing one can do. The landlord has unrestricted right of access to those parts of the house which are common to all the tenants.'

'Does Mr Riscock ever appear himself?'

'No. He has a thuggish young aide who is graced with the title of clerk of the works and he's the most frequent visitor. He's a brash, graceless young man with an ability to intimidate the faint-hearted.'

'But not you or Judge Kilby?'

'I make a point of not letting him see my feelings. As for Judge Kilby, I suspect she would gladly have despatched him to prison if she'd had the opportunity. He certainly failed to intimidate her.'

'What's his name?'

'He's always referred to as Jez. Don't ask me what it's short for, because I've no idea. I merely assume it's not Jezebel.'

Chantry glanced about the room. 'Do you know whether the building is still considered safe?'

'I spoke to someone from the Borough Surveyor's department shortly before you came and he said he didn't think the house was in any danger of collapse, but that if one had somewhere else to go he would advise it.'

'It must have been an alarming experience,' Chantry said, glancing about him.

'It was certainly a very loud bang and then all the noise of breaking glass, followed by clouds of choking dust. Mr Gilfroy thought it was the end of the world; an event he's been expecting in the wake of Halley's Comet.'

'Well, thank you for your help, Miss Cherry.' Chantry paused. 'I know you've been asked this before, but do you have any fresh ideas about Judge Kilby's murder?'

'None,' she said, shaking her head. 'We were never on particularly close terms and I didn't know her friends – or her enemies.'

After bidding her farewell, the two officers picked their way across the debris-strewn hall to the front door which hung askew.

An overweight, tough-looking young man was gesticulating to a constable out on the drive.

'Looks as if that could be Jez,' Chantry observed.

As they approached, they heard him say, 'Bloody hopeless

mob, that's what they are. Call themselves fitters! I wouldn't trust them to buy a packet of cigarettes. More than likely they'd come back with yesterday's paper.'

'Are you Jez?'

'Yep. And who are you?'

'Detective Chief Inspector Chantry.'

Jez's eyes narrowed. 'Seem to have heard the name somewhere. I was just telling your bloke here what a bloody dangerous lot these gas fitters are.' He let out a hoarse chuckle. 'If they'd been around at the time, they'd have made a much better job blowing up the Houses of Parliament than that poor sod, Guy Fawkes, did. "Leave it to us, Guy," they'd more than likely have told him.'

'Finished?'

Jez shot Chantry a look of instant dislike.

'And if I have?'

'I understand you were here on the afternoon the leak was detected by Miss Cherry.'

'Correct. I went up to take a look at the roof. Spoke to Mrs Ives, if you want to know. But I assure you there wasn't any smell of gas while I was at the house.'

'Did you go down to the basement?'

'Had no reason to.'

'But did you?'

'No, I did not. And you can stop your insinuating.'

'So no chance we'd find your fingerprints down there?'

Jez's jaw dropped. 'I've been down there often,' he said truculently. 'But not that afternoon.'

'Well, stay away until I say you can come back.'

'Look, mate, I take my orders from Mr Riscock and no one else.'

'Get moving, sonny,' Chantry said with a sneer. 'And, while you're at it, you can tell Mr Riscock I'll want to see him later in the day.'

Jez scowled and turned abruptly away. As Chantry watched him go over to his car – a well-used-looking Mercedes – the question that occupied his mind was, if the explosion had been deliberately caused, was the intention merely to dislodge the

120

tenants or was there some deeper motive related to Judge Kilby's murder?

Chantry decided that a police station would provide a more persuasive atmosphere for interviewing Bernard Riscock. Accordingly, he despatched Sergeant Kirkbride and a detective constable to escort him back to the divisional headquarters where he had set up his own base.

Riscock had his own ideas, however, and was out when the officers arrived. He had left a message to say that if Detective Chief Inspector Chantry wished to see him, he should make an appointment with his solicitor who would accompany him to any interview.

When Kirkbride returned and reported this, Chantry looked pensive for a moment of two.

'He's not being very sensible,' he said after a while. 'But then big-heads like him seldom are. Next time we'll just grab him.' Observing Kirkbride's expression he went on, 'As soon as we know for certain that the explosion was deliberately caused, we'll bring Riscock in for questioning, if necessary kicking and screaming all the way. I spoke to one of the Gas Board's accident inspectors while you were out and he's pretty sure it must have been deliberate. It seems that the piece of new pipe fitted two days ago showed signs of having been tampered with.'

'Does he have any idea how the gas was ignited?'

'Amongst the debris in the cellar was one of those old-fashioned gas pokers. The theory is that it was lit and placed some distance from the leak. Then as the level of escaping gas built up, the explosion occurred.'

'That means Jez or somebody must have been down in the basement only shortly beforehand.'

Chantry nodded. 'I've ascertained that Jez was one of the first people to arrive at the scene. He tried to go down to the basement, but was prevented. He explained his presence by saying that he'd heard about the earlier leak and wanted to satisfy himself that everything was now all right.'

'Did he also explain why he was up and about so early?'

'He even answered that before the question was asked. He

121

was on his way from his home in Merton to Riscock's office, where he always arrives by eight o'clock. It required only a minor detour to call in at Aubusson Way.'

'He seems to have thought of everything.'

'Almost everything,' Chantry remarked. 'He forgot his gloves. At least, I hope we can prove they're his. A pair was found in the basement close to where the gas poker was lying. They had grease marks on the fingers of one hand. It could be grease from the newly fitted pipe.'

'Who discovered the gloves?'

'Sergeant Booth from the local station who was one of the first to arrive at the scene. I spoke to him while you were out.'

'The gloves could have been down there for ages,' Kirkbride said doubtfully.

'They were almost new.'

'If they were Jez's, why should he have taken them off?'

'I've thought of the answer to that, too,' Chantry said. 'He undoubtedly wore them to avoid leaving fingerprints, but also because he was doing a mucky job. Did you notice his hands when we were talking to him, Bill? Nicely manicured nails. Not the hands of a manual worker, whatever the rest of his appearance.'

'So why did he take the gloves off?'

'If you'd ever tried to light one of those old-fashioned gas pokers, you'd know how easily you could use up a whole box of matches, particularly if it was turned on low. Remember, the gas would already have been escaping on the other side of the basement and Jez would have been anxious not to blow himself up, too. It would have been a race against time. If I'm right, he took off his gloves to light the poker, which he presumably did with a cigarette lighter. Try operating a cigarette lighter with a pair of commercial gloves on! Anyway, having removed them and got the poker alight, it's not hard to imagine his forgetting to pick them up in his haste to get away.'

Sergeant Kirkbride grinned. 'That's very ingenious, sir. I shall enjoy seeing Jez sweat a bit. Assuming you're right, where does that leave Riscock in relation to Judge Kilby's murder?'

'Anyone who's capable of blowing up a house with people

inside is capable of arranging a murder. Riscock's a totally ruthless operator and he was obviously determined to get vacant possession of the property. Fair means having failed, he resorted to foul.'

'But why destroy his own property?'

'I imagine he'd be quite happy to have the house condemned as unsafe, because then he'll be able to erect something even more valuable on the site. Moreover, I have no doubt it's well insured. He probably thought he was on to a winner whatever happened.' Chantry gave his sergeant a small, complacent smile. 'With a bit of luck, we're going to put him behind bars for a long time. Even for life, if we can do him for murder.'

CHAPTER 23

Rosa had not seen Peter Chen since she'd cooked him dinner on Saturday evening. The next day he had flown off to Kuwait on a brief business trip, returning late Wednesday night. He had called her immediately he got back, suggesting he should come round, but Rosa, who was already in bed, had demurred. She pointed out that they had a dinner date for the following evening and that she needed her beauty sleep.

'How was Kuwait?' she enquired.

'Almost as many Arabs there as in London,' he said. 'But I want to hear about your case. What's been happening while I was away?'

'Peter Duxbury got bail and today there's been a serious explosion at Judge Kilby's house. Those are the main developments.'

'How was your meeting with Crowhurst?'

'I'll tell you about that when I see you tomorrow.'

'And what about Judge K's mysterious friend in Sussex?'

'I'll tell you about him, too, tomorrow. Not that there's very much to tell.'

'Are you looking forward to seeing me again?'

Rosa laughed. 'It'd serve you right if I said no.'

'That would cause me to lose face,' he said gravely.

123

'Better face than fortune.'

'That's a very materialistic thing to say. Perhaps I'd better come over . . .'

'If you don't let me get to sleep, I shall look a wreck tomorrow.'

'You couldn't.'

Rosa sighed. She knew from past experience that he was capable of keeping a conversation going all night.

'Pick me up at seven-thirty tomorrow evening,' she said firmly. 'And Peter?'

'Yes.'

'Of course I'm looking forward to seeing you again. Very much, if you must know.'

'Good night, little Rosa,' he said softly and rang off. She could picture his cherubic smile. Like most men, he was vain and quietly enjoyed being flattered.

She was ready and waiting when he arrived the next evening. She had chosen to wear a brilliant red skirt and a white silk blouse with puff sleeves and a large, floppy bow that matched the skirt.

'Stunning,' he said, standing back and gazing at her when she opened the door. Then he stepped quickly forward and gave her a delicate kiss that confirmed her pleasure at seeing him again. 'A present from Kuwait,' he said, handing her a small, gift-wrapped box.

'What can it be?' Rosa said, giving it a small shake to see if it rattled.

She opened it carefully to avoid tearing the attractive wrapping paper and gave a gasp of delight when she saw the contents, a pair of emerald earrings.

'Oh, Peter, they're beautiful. But not even you can afford to be so generous. Nevertheless, thank you very much, indeed.' She gave him a quick kiss. 'I shall put them on straight away. Did they really come from Kuwait?'

'There's nothing you can't get at the Duty Free,' he said with a grin. 'Now let's go, as I want to hear all about everything. I've booked a table at the Mirabelle.'

124

'Emerald earrings *and* dinner at the Mirabelle,' Rosa said with a happy smile.

'My client in Kuwait was pleased with recent advice I'd given him and added a nought to his cheque.'

Rosa laughed. 'Talk about fat cats and church mice in the same profession.'

They arrived at the restaurant and found a secluded corner in the bar. Rosa ordered a campari soda, a drink she normally associated with holidays and Peter had his usual whisky and water.

'Now tell me what's been happening in your case,' he said, when their drinks had arrived. 'So Duxbury got bail? Did you have to fight hard?'

'No, I think they'd made up their minds that unless the police came up with something fresh, they'd grant bail. As it was, Chantry could only repeat what he'd said the previous week.'

'They're clearly no closer to charging Duxbury with murder, then.'

'It seems not. Thank goodness!'

'You feel more kindly towards him now?' Peter enquired.

'Not really.'

'You said, thank goodness.'

'I was thinking of Chantry, whom I like. He'd be making real trouble for himself if he charged Peter Duxbury with the murder. I'm more than ever convinced he didn't do it.'

'So who did?'

'The police are trying to trace Edward Maxwell, that's her friend who lives in Sussex. But he's disappeared. At least, he's gone away and nobody seems to know when he'll be back. It's significant that he went off three days after the murder and didn't tell his staff where he was going or when to expect his return.'

'How did you find all this out?'

'Frank Petro told me his name, so I looked him up in the telephone directory and found he lives at a place called Brake's Farm. I phoned there yesterday evening and a woman with not very good English answered. I asked if I could speak to Mrs

Maxwell and was told there was no Mrs Maxwell and that Mr Maxwell lived alone. The woman said that she and her husband were the only staff and that their name was da Costa.'

'Sounds Portuguese. How did you manage to get so much information out of her?'

'I said I was doing a market research survey of farms in West Sussex for a fertiliser firm.'

'And she actually believed you?'

'I told her we were giving away valuable prizes to specially selected customers and that she qualified for one.'

'Crafty little Rosa! But now you'll have to send her something.'

'I've already done so. A head scarf I was given last Christmas and have never worn. It's black with a hideous fluorescent orange pattern.'

'That'll curdle the cows' milk.'

'But I need to know more about Edward Maxwell, Peter,' Rosa went on earnestly. 'Why's he chosen this moment to disappear?'

'Did you ask Mrs da Costa whether she knew Judge Kilby?'

Rosa shook her head. 'It was a bit difficult to ask that as part of my fertiliser sales talk.'

Peter looked thoughtful. 'I could drive down tomorrow and see if I could dig out a bit more. Shall I do that?'

'What would be your excuse for a visit?'

He gave a shrug. 'I could say that a friend of Mr Maxwell's has told me he's interested in Chinese ceramics and that happens to be my line of business. Anyway, a cover story won't present any problems.' He frowned in thought before continuing. 'I wonder whether Judge Kilby's will will contain any clues. The police must have thought of that. After all, wills provide endless motives for bad feeling and skullduggery.'

'I got Robin to phone Bleck and Co who were her solicitors. He used to sit on some committee or other with Percy Bleck, the senior partner. He was told she'd left almost everything to charity.'

'To make up for her absence of it when she was alive, I suppose,' Peter observed. 'Didn't she have any family?'

126

'Only an illegitimate son,' Rosa said, and went on to tell him what she had been able to learn about Tony Kilby.

'He sounds as good a suspect as any.'

'He receives only a small legacy under his mother's will.'

'Even so.'

'I gather the police are satisfied he's in the clear.'

'Don't forget, the same police were equally sure of Duxbury's guilt.'

'I know. I'd quite like to talk to Tony Kilby myself. I've written to ask him to get in touch with me. So far without result.'

'We can go and seek him out together.'

Rosa nodded abstractedly. 'I think I'm more interested in Edward Maxwell.'

'What would his motive have been?'

'I've no idea. But as long as he remains an unknown quantity, he could have all sorts of motives.'

Peter ordered a further round of drinks while he and Rosa began to study the menus they'd been handed. After they had chosen (scampi mornay for Rosa and a tournedos for him, in each case preceded by smoked salmon mousse) he said, 'Didn't you say something last night about an explosion at the judge's house?'

'Yes, it happened early yesterday morning. I drove up there in the evening after leaving the office. There are hardly any windows left and I should think the foundations may have been damaged. I spoke to one of the tenants, a Miss Cherry, and she was in no doubt it had been deliberately caused and that their landlord was behind it. I gather the police are concentrating their attention on him.'

'They think he did the murder?'

'I imagine they have that in mind.'

'He strikes me as a less likely suspect than the illegitimate son.'

'I agree,' Rosa said in a thoughtful voice. 'If it'd been he who stabbed her in the back on a dark Saturday night, he'd never have bothered to pin a melodramatic note to her body. Also he'd have been more likely to have coshed her.' She paused. 'I

127

think that note tells us quite a lot about the murderer. It shows he had vengeance high on his agenda.'

'I wonder if Edward Maxwell fits that bill?'

'So do I.'

'All the more reason for me to go down to Horsham tomorrow.'

'Don't forget to take your samples with you.'

'Samples? What samples?'

'A selection of Ming vases,' Rosa said, suddenly aware that she was feeling light-headed.

At that moment, the maitre d' glided forward to say that their table was ready.

When they were seated and their first course had arrived, Peter said, 'Tell me about your visit to Giles Crowhurst.'

Rosa had, meanwhile, drunk a glass of iced water and decided to go easy on the wine.

'I felt rather sorry for him,' she said. 'He's got a kindly face, but gives the impression of having been unfairly buffeted by life. He made no secret of the fact that he'd been in love with Celia Kilby.'

'Sounds a born masochist. Did he tell you anything useful?'

'He thought the landlord, Bernard Riscock, had both the motive and the ability to have arranged for her demise. And that, of course, was before yesterday's explosion.'

'Did he have any other suspect?'

'He mentioned Edward Maxwell, though not by name. He said he was aware she'd been spending weekends in Sussex with a friend and was convinced it was a man.'

'Did he seem jealous?'

'No, just resigned. Apparently, she had rebuffed him sharply when he tried to find out who the friend was.'

'Could he have killed her? He seems to have had motive enough.'

'If you're referring to unrequited love, that had been going on for years. Moreover, she had recently helped him get a job with the EEC in Brussels. She gave him the necessary reference.'

'Did he tell you that himself?'

'No, I learnt it only today. I tried to phone him at his Chambers and discovered that the new number two clerk there had come from Chambers I often use. Anyway, I congratulated him on his promotion, he was third clerk in his old Chambers, and we had a bit of a gossip. He told me Giles Crowhurst was off to Brussels at the end of the month and had gone over for a few days to look for a flat and have a general look around. He added that Mr Crowhurst had been given a testimonial by Judge Kilby only shortly before her death and wasn't that fortunate?' Rosa paused and went on, 'It rather shows that Crowhurst was finally giving up the chase and that Judge Kilby was prepared to help him move out of her orbit.'

'Sounds typical of the lady! I bet she was thinking more of helping herself than assisting him.'

'It looks that way and yet . . .'

'And yet what?'

'I don't really know. Typical in one way, but untypical in another.'

Peter peered approvingly at the tournedos that had just been put in front of him.

'At least there's one thing that can be ruled out,' he said, 'and that's suicide.'

Rosa bit into a delicious cheese-flavoured scampi.

'I'll tell you something else,' she said. 'This food is far too good to be accompanied by talk of sordid murder.'

Peter cast her a surprised look. 'If I didn't know you better, I might think you were being serious. But OK, let's talk about where we're going on holiday.'

'I hadn't realised we'd got as far as where. I thought we still had to decide whether.'

He shook his head. 'No, it's where, followed by when. Or, if you prefer, when, followed by where.'

CHAPTER 24

Bernard Riscock had been at the station thirty-six hours, helping police with their enquiries. At least, that was how his

129

detention was formally described. In reality he had spent the greater part of the time sitting in surly silence while his solicitor, Felix Hartman, sweated profusely and hopped about like an angry chipmunk. He was someone who perspired freely in all weathers as he went about his clients' business with expressions of indignation and outrage. These emotional explosions were the screen behind which a coolly calculating mind functioned.

Chantry had never been hopeful of breaking Riscock's resistance and obtaining a confession, but it had been a necessary exercise and nothing had been lost. The next day, however, he would have either to be charged or released. To obtain approval for a further twenty-four hours' detention would serve no purpose, apart from making Riscock even angrier. Though Chantry found that a tempting objective

Experts from the Gas Board and from the police laboratory were now ready to testify that the explosion must have been deliberately caused. If that were so, there was only one person who had an interest in causing it.

To add to suspicion, Jez had disappeared. 'Gone on holiday,' Riscock had said and gone on saying. 'Where?' Chantry had asked and gone on asking. The answer was that his employer had no idea and didn't care.

Chantry felt reasonably confident, however, that Jez would be flushed from his cover before long, and, when that happened, he would find himself facing a tough and relentless interrogation. The police were not without ammunition to fire at him. There were the gloves discovered at the scene of the explosion, which scientific evidence should be able to relate to him once they had some control samples from Jez himself. There was also the business card of a garage which had been found amongst the debris in the basement. It turned out to be the garage that serviced Jez's car. Chantry assumed it had had some impromptu part in the preparations for the explosion, but it was something else that called for an explanation.

Thus, the hunt for Jez was on and, when found, Chantry hoped he'd be able to frighten him into incriminating Riscock. From his single brief encounter with Jez, he had the impression of a fast-talking bully, but not someone who would have any difficulty choosing between loyalty to his boss and saving his own skin.

Chantry rose and walked across to the window, from which he had a framed view of the New Tandoori Restaurant, N. K. Gupta's Grocery Store and the surgery of M. Malhotra, dental surgeon.

His mind, however, was not on things Indian. He was thinking of Peter Duxbury who was charged with sending Judge Kilby a letter threatening to murder her and of Bernard Riscock whom he hoped soon to charge with causing criminal damage to the house in which the judge had lived. But still he lacked the evidence to charge anyone with the actual murder.

In a moment of despondency, he wondered if the crime would ever be solved. It was frustrating enough to know the identity of a murderer and not be able to charge him for want of evidence. Even worse, however, was to be in total darkness as to a killer's identity. It was like being surrounded and mocked by malign spirits.

Or so it seemed to Chief Inspector Chantry at the end of another long day.

When the phone rang, Maria de Costa and her husband both stared at it with suspicion. They were in their flat above the stables which had a separate line from the main house, but few people knew the number and it wasn't often they received calls. For Maria, the telephone was well down on her list of desirable amenities. In fact, she would have been happier without it, save when her family in Portugal congregated in her cousin's café and spoke to her in turn. But that was always on a Sunday night and this was only Friday.

Her husband gestured her to answer it.

''Allo,' she said stiffly, holding the receiver away from her ear.

'Maria, it's Mr Maxwell,' he said, speaking in Portuguese. His father had been an English lawyer with a practice in Lisbon and Edward had grown up bilingual. He still spoke the language

131

with reasonable fluency. It was his affinity with Portugal that had caused him to engage a couple from that country to look after his home.

'Mr Maxwell, I am so glad that you phone,' Maria said with a surge of relief at hearing his voice and being able to converse in her mother tongue.

'Is everything all right?' he asked, alerted by her tone.

'Yes, but so many people wanting you and the police . . .'

'The police? What did they want?'

'They were wishing to know where you are and when you are coming back. I tell them I don't know.'

'Did they say why they wanted to see me?'

'No, they just ask a lot of questions. They were police from London,' she added nervously.

'Tell me exactly what they asked you, Maria.'

'They asked if I knew about Juiz Keelby who is killed, but I tell them I knew nothing. They ask if she stayed here at weekends, but I tell them again it is none of my business and I know nothing.'

'I see. How many police officers were there?'

'Only one. Also he is quite a gentleman.'

Maxwell found no particular reassurance in this testimonial.

'How long did he stay?'

'Thirty minutes perhaps.'

'Did he want to look over the house?'

'No. He go away after I tell him you are not here and I don't know when you'll be back.'

'When did he come?'

'Last Monday.'

'Has anyone else been asking for me?'

'A Chinese man came this morning. He had fine Chinese objects to sell.'

'What on earth are you talking about, Maria?'

'Chinese porcelain,' Maria said anxiously. 'He thought you would like to buy.'

'Did he say why he'd chosen to call at Brake's Farm?' Maxwell asked in a restrained tone.

'He had been given your name.'

132

'Did he ask any questions about me personally?'

'I tell him nothing,' Maria said quickly, and untruthfully.

In fact she had been totally charmed by Peter Chen, who had made her laugh and turned their encounter into a sort of amusing game. He used to good effect the two dozen words or so of Portuguese he had picked up on visits to Macao. When she mentioned that her employer spoke excellent Portuguese and knew that country well, her visitor seemed particularly interested. Mr Maxwell's tone, however, warned her that discretion was the better part of valour.

'When are you coming home, sir?' she now asked quickly, hoping to divert him from further questions about Peter Chen.

'I'm not sure,' he replied. 'But I'd sooner you didn't talk to anyone while I'm away. Do you understand, Maria?'

'Of course. I speak to nobody. But if the police call again . . . They wanted very much to see you . . .'

'Just tell them you don't know when I'll be back. After all that's the truth, isn't it? And you know that the Blessed Virgin whose name you bear always wants you to tell the truth.'

'*Sim, sim,*' she said, hastily crossing herself.

'As long as you and Luiz take care of Brake's Farm, I'll be pleased. But no more talking about me to strangers. And tell Luiz to chop up that fallen tree for winter logs.'

'He already does so.'

'Excellent. I'll arrange for some money to be sent to you, so no need to worry about that either.'

A moment later he had said goodbye and rung off.

Luiz who had been listening with frowning attention, now said, 'Where was he?'

'How should I know? He didn't say.'

'You should have asked him.'

'If he'd wanted me to know, he'd have said. It doesn't do to be inquisitive.'

Luiz shook his head in obvious doubt. He was less bright than his wife and accepted her advice in most things. He was uneasy, however, over their employer's abrupt departure from Brake's Farm, followed by a visit from the police. And then there was some judge who'd been murdered . . .

He couldn't make sense of any of it, but it was a worrying situation.

As it happened, this was also Edward Maxwell's considered view. He had phoned from the apartment in Lisbon which was still family property, though normally let. Its tenant of the past twenty years had died earlier that year and it had since lain unoccupied. In the circumstances, it seemed the obvious place to go when he decided to get out of England for a while. Nobody at home was aware of its existence, though there was a reference to it in his will. But surely his solicitor would never divulge such information however pressing the police became . . .

He'd kept in touch with current developments in the hunt for Celia Kilby's killer by reading all the English papers he could lay his hands on and by listening to the BBC World Service. He was aware that the police wished to interview him and had appealed for him to come forward. Of course, as he was abroad, there was no reason why he should be expected to know what was going on at home. Nevertheless his conversation with Maria had unsettled him.

The police had long arms these days and although he didn't expect to be suddenly arrested (how could he be arrested without evidence?), the possibility remained that they might come knocking on his door with courteous smiles and awkward questions.

Perhaps he ought to leave Lisbon before his welcome turned sour.

Perhaps a short visit to one of the countries of South or Central America would be advisable.

But suddenly he checked his flow of thoughts in alarm, as he realised he was already beginning to think like a fugitive from justice.

And all because of a woman who had led him up the garden path and then got herself murdered.

Maybe he should return home and face the music, and really help the police with their enquiries.

* * *

134

Peter Duxbury knew that Rosa had been right when she said that he would remain under a cloud of suspicion until somebody had been charged and convicted of the murder. It was a truth he regarded as utterly intolerable.

After three days of regained liberty, his morale had risen and he was once more feeling his assertive self.

He had spoken on the phone to the head of his Chambers and been advised against showing his face in the Temple for the time being. Though expressed in sympathetic terms, the message had been unmistakable and had increased his general feeling of resentment. It had certainly added to his already considerable sense of injustice. Like many who are self-assured, he expected everyone to see things as he saw them. In his case, that meant recognising the letter he had sent Judge Kilby as nothing more than an indiscretion. With hindsight he realised it would have been better not to have sent it (and, of course, he had never admitted doing so other than to his solicitor), but it was absurd to have taken it so seriously. As for keeping him in custody for a week, that had been a monstrous act and something he wouldn't readily forgive or forget. It made him even more determined to clear his name. He was so obsessed with the thought that he found it easy to overlook the fact he already stood charged with one criminal offence. But that anyone could possibly suspect him of murder was an outrageous slur and he was resolved to vindicate his honour.

With these thoughts seething in his mind, he had spent three days preparing himself for direct action. After a careful sifting of all the information at his disposal, he had no doubt who had killed Judge Kilby. Indeed, he had felt near-certainty from the moment when Rosa had told him of the existence of the judge's illegitimate son, who had recently returned from Australia and was actually the last known person to see her alive. The police might accept that he had a satisfactory alibi, but he, Peter Duxbury, saw this as a further example of their refusal to look beyond himself for the murderer. He estimated that it would have been perfectly possible for Kilby, after saying good night to his mother, to have dashed off and reached Aubusson Way before she got there. All he then had to do was to lie in wait and kill her after she had put her car in its garage. And when it came to motive, whose were stronger than her estranged and illegitimate son's . . .?

It had taken him only half a day to trace the hotel in Earl's Court where Kilby was staying and he had spent the past two days keeping him under observation. This, in practice, meant following him from the hotel to a nearby pub twice a day and back again, with occasional inbetween visits to a pizza joint that lay on his route.

He had the impression that his quarry was engaged in a waiting game of some sort. Each day was an exercise in killing time. He appeared not to have any friends, although he usually fell into conversation with people in the pub.

Duxbury decided to make his strike on Saturday evening. He hoped that after several pints of beer Kilby's tongue would be loose and that a sudden confrontation would take him by surprise so that he would be drawn into a damaging admission about his mother's death.

Determined not to miss him when he left the seedy hotel where he was staying, he arrived early and took up a position about thirty yards from its entrance. Kilby normally left around seven o'clock for his evening visit to the pub.

It was a street of shabby, terraced houses, most of which had been converted into short-lease flats, with the occasional bed and breakfast establishment sandwiched in between. It was a district with a transient population that came from every point of the compass, where nobody paid much attention to his neighbour. Although it bristled with young people of Duxbury's own age, he felt a complete alien. It was a scene far removed from the staid atmosphere of the Temple in which he felt at home.

Much to his relief, Anthony Kilby emerged from the hotel a few minutes after seven and headed for the pub. He had been worried lest Saturday night might bring a change of routine, but apparently not. Kilby was dressed in the same faded jeans and zip-up black windcheater he'd worn before. He had a tough, self-contained look, although Duxbury had seen him in amiable conversation with fellow drinkers. Nevertheless, he always returned to the hotel on his own when the pub closed; though the previous evening he had tried, albeit unsuccessfully, to pick up a girl on his way back. For all Duxbury knew, he might emerge again later in a more predatory frame of mind.

By the time Peter Duxbury reached the pub, Kilby already had a pint of draught bitter in front of him and was chatting to the darker of the two barmaids who, with a peroxided blond young man and the publican himself, made up the staff. He ordered a brandy and soda and went to sit in a corner from where he could observe everything that went on.

After about half an hour, Kilby, who was then on his second pint of beer, moved along the bar to where two girls were on their own. They appeared to accept his company as a tolerable distraction. Duxbury hoped he wouldn't get too involved with them as he relied on Kilby leaving the pub alone as he had done the previous evenings.

By eight-thirty the pub was packed with an influx of Saturday night drinkers. Duxbury would have liked another drink himself, but didn't dare leave his strategic corner, knowing his seat would be taken before he was half-way to the bar. The only consolation was that he had bought himself a double in the first place.

He noticed that one of the girls to whom Kilby was talking was staring about her with a bored expression. Her companion, however, seemed to be hanging on his every word. Even as he watched they were joined by two young men. Introductions were made, but ten minutes later the girls departed with the new arrivals.

Kilby glanced at his watch and seemed to be weighing up whether he had time for another drink before making his own departure. With an air of sudden decision he put his empty glass down on the counter and began to thrust his way towards the door.

Taken somewhat by surprise, Duxbury, who had never seen him leave before closing time, sprang up to follow him. He had a moment of panic on reaching the pavement and losing sight of his quarry. Then he saw him crossing the road twenty yards away and hurried after him. Muttering cursory apologies to people whom he bumped into, he closed the distance between them. It seemed that after all Kilby was returning to his hotel. Perhaps he was due at a Saturday night party later on.

This was confirmed when Kilby dived into an off-licence. From the pavement, Peter Duxbury saw him select a bottle of Spanish red wine and half a dozen large cans of beer from the shelf and pay for them. He drew back when Kilby emerged with his purchases and gave him a ten yard start.

As they turned into the road where the hotel was located, he shortened the distance between them. When he was only three yards behind he called out in a commanding voice: 'Stop!'

Kilby did so, turned and glared.

'I want to have a word with you,' Duxbury went on.

'Who the hell are you? You've been following me around, haven't you? I saw you yesterday and in the pub this evening and it must have been you who was asking about me at the hotel.'

As he spoke, he rested the bag containing the drink on the ground between his feet.

'You're Kilby, aren't you?' Duxbury said aggressively. 'I want to have a quiet word with you. Now.'

Kilby looked momentarily taken aback at being so peremptorily addressed.

'What about?' he said suspiciously.

'I know you murdered your mother, so admit it,' Duxbury said in a tone of hectoring cross-examination.

For a second or two Kilby just stared at him in disbelief. Then he said viciously, 'You'd better sod off or you'll suffer the same fate.'

To underline his message, his fist shot out and caught Duxbury a severe blow on the side of his chin. He fell heavily to the ground and it was several seconds before he picked himself up and leaned groggily against some railings. Kilby had, meanwhile, vanished.

Peter Duxbury decided it was time to go home and consider his next move. Despite the indignity of being knocked to the ground, he was not displeased with his evening's work.

Kilby's violent reaction could only be seen as an admission of his mother's murder.

CHAPTER 25

Rosa spent Sunday at Robin's. She arrived in time for family lunch and stayed till early evening. He lived with his wife, Susan, and two children not far from Heathrow airport. It was an Elizabethan house with a rambling garden, with only the planes to disturb its peace, which they did constantly and effectively. But the Snaiths had lived there since before World War II and Robin had been born in the house. As a consequence they had grown used to the noise and it was only their visitors who were apt to stare at the ceiling in alarm as if expecting a landing wheel to come ripping through the plaster every time a plane passed overhead.

Rosa and Susan had always got on well and the children enjoyed her visits, though the days when she used to read to them had long passed. Now it was games of Trivial Pursuit and knock-out whist that brought them round the table after lunch.

Rosa had come to regard them as part of her own family and never felt more relaxed than when sharing their company.

It was nearing the time of her departure when she and Robin found themselves alone for the first time that day. Susan was attending to some chore upstairs and the children had gone off to a neighbour's house. Almost inevitably their conversation turned to the Kilby case.

Although she often argued with him, Rosa had a great respect for her senior partner's judgment; not to mention gratitude for the endless patience he always showed her.

'It might be worth your going to see the surviving members of that bridge four,' he said suddenly in a ruminative tone.

'I've talked to Giles Crowhurst.' Rosa replied.

'I know you have. I was really thinking of that woman. What's her name? Mrs Spenser, is it?'

'Spicer. Adèle Spicer.'

'A chat with her might bring dividends.'

Rosa gave him a quizzical look. 'What is it you have in mind, Robin?'

'I'm sure you're right in believing that the murderer will be found in Judge Kilby's social circle and it occurs to me that Mrs Spicer might be able to give you a fresh slant on that.'

'It's worth a try,' Rosa remarked. 'I'll call her tomorrow.'

'The trouble is that the case has thrown up so many red herrings and, as I'm frequently saying, you can often only identify a red herring in retrospect.'

'Like Edward Maxwell,' Rosa said. 'Which is he? Red herring or murderer?'

Robin nodded. 'Could be either. The most significant thing about him is the timing of his disappearance. He's obviously a person of substance and some standing, so why should he have run away like a frightened schoolboy?' He paused. 'Except, of course, you and I both know that even the brightest among us is capable of irrational conduct.'

Rosa became thoughtful and when she spoke again it was with a note of hesitation.

'You don't mind my continuing to spend time on the case, do you, Robin?'

'Why should I mind?'

'Because, strictly speaking, it's not my business. My only concern is to defend Peter Duxbury on the charge of sending a letter threatening to murder.'

'I realise that, but, as I see it, that charge and Judge Kilby's murder are inextricably linked, even if they were committed by two different people. Chantry's line of enquiry has ensured that.'

'Thank you,' Rosa said with a grateful smile. 'I was beginning to feel a bit guilty.'

'In any event,' Robin went on, 'it seems to me that most of your sleuthing has been conducted outside office hours.'

'Then I shall try and see Adèle Spicer at cocktail time,' she said cheerfully.

A little later she made her departure, after thanking Robin and Susan warmly for their hospitality. As usual, Susan sent her on her way with beans and courgettes from the garden and two pots of homemade marmalade.

Rosa hadn't been home more than a few minutes when her phone rang. She thought it was probably Peter Chen calling to ask her out for a drink.

'Ah, so you're back,' a voice said querulously. It took her a

140

moment to realise that it was the other Peter in her life. Peter Duxbury.

'I didn't recognise your voice immediately,' she said. 'You sound different.'

'I have a very sore face. I can't talk properly. I was viciously assaulted last night. I've been trying to call you all day to tell you what happened.'

'What did happen?' Rosa asked with a sinking heart.

Peter Duxbury gave her a full account of events and concluded, 'The police clearly need to investigate Kilby much more thoroughly than they've troubled to do so far. I'd like you to pass on to Chantry what I've said and tell him to think again.'

'You want *me* to?' Rosa said in a startled voice.

'Yes. It'll come better from you. They're likely to pay more attention if it comes with your backing.'

'They'll still need a statement from you before they take any action on the assault.'

'I'm not interested in the assault, as such, even though it did occasion me actual bodily harm within the meaning of the section. What the police have got to do is get off their backsides and investigate Kilby as the probable murderer of his mother. It's not good enough to accept his alibi without question.'

'How do you know they haven't tested it and found that it stands up?' Rosa asked, somewhat stung by her client's presumptive tone.

'Look at the time Chantry's spent hounding me!' Duxbury said indignantly.'Moreover, I don't see how anyone can have a watertight alibi for the murder unless they were out of the country at the time. There's no way they can pinpoint the actual time it was committed. It's mere assumption that she was killed after driving home that evening. Her body wasn't found until nearly eight o'clock on Sunday morning. Who's to say she went straight home after leaving the restaurant where she had dinner?'

'It's a reasonable inference, seeing that nobody's come forward to say otherwise.' Duxbury gave a scornful laugh and Rosa went on, 'Moreover, if she didn't go straight home, it refutes your theory that it was her son who killed her.'

'Not at all,' he said in a tone of superior knowledge. 'I should have thought it was also obvious he had the clearest motive of anyone.'

'How do you work that out?'

'He'd been appallingly treated by that monster of a woman who was his mother and it's plain that, on the night they met, something happened between them that proved to be the straw that broke the camel's back. Possibly she told him that she had cut him out of the will, apart from a small legacy. There's motive for you!'

'Surely it would have been a stronger motive if she'd told him he'd inherit the lot on her death?'

'Perhaps that's what the duplicitous woman did tell him.'

'This is all guesswork on your part,' Rosa said after a pause. 'And pretty wild guesswork at that.'

'It's not guesswork that I was grievously assaulted last night.'

'I'm talking about the so-called motives you attribute to him. They just don't make sense.'

'That's only because we don't know what took place when they had dinner that night.'

Rosa sighed. She realised that nothing she said would cause Peter Duxbury to change his mind.

'Let me think about what you've said and speak to you again in a day or two,' she said peaceably.

'I definitely want you to pass on my views to the police. After all, it was you yourself who told me I'd remain under suspicion until the true murderer had been arrested for all the world to see.'

'I know I did and I'm afraid it's so.'

It struck her as ironic that one moment he was portraying Anthony Kilby as someone capable of vicious matricide and the next as the most injured of all injured parties.

As she was still sitting beside the phone after their conversation had ended she decided to call Adèle Spicer. She found her number in the directory and was agreeably surprised when Mrs Spicer promptly answered.

Rosa introduced herself and asked if she might visit her. Mrs Spicer said she already knew Rosa by name and would be delighted to meet her for a chat about poor Celia Kilby's tragic death.

After she had rung off, Rosa began to wonder which of them would pump the other with the greater vigour. Adèle Spicer clearly expected Rosa to have nuggets of information not revealed to the public at large. Equally, however, she appeared to be longing to talk to someone about her dear friend. Rosa wasn't to know that she felt slighted by police lack of interest in her. One brief visit from a junior officer was all she had been accorded.

It was Rosa's hope, albeit an outside one, that if Mrs Spicer talked long enough, some small clue to Judge Kilby's death might emerge.

CHAPTER 26

Rosa arrived at Adèle Spicer's flat on the dot of six-thirty the next evening. She lived on the top floor of an expensive block with a panoramic view over Wimbledon Common. A melodious chime sounded somewhere inside when Rosa pressed the doorbell. She heard footsteps and was aware of somebody observing her through the spy-hole before the door was opened.

'Do come in, dear,' Mrs Spicer said with a welcoming smile. She was wearing a billowing pale-green dress and smelt delicately of talcum powder.

Rosa followed her into the spacious living-room whose predominant feature was bright chintzes.

'I love bright colours,' her hostess said, observing Rosa's glance about the room. 'So much of life is drab and ugly these days that I try and surround myself with cheerful things. Now, dear, what will you have? I'm a gin person myself, but I have a well-stocked bar so make your choice.'

'Would it be possible to have a glass of white wine?'

'Of course. I should have guessed. It's the in-drink amongst young people these days, isn't it? I know my nephew and his friends always drink it.'

'I quite often drink other things,' Rosa said, not wishing to be so instantly categorised. 'It's just that I feel like wine this evening if it's not giving you too much trouble.'

'No trouble at all, dear.' Mrs Spicer poured the drinks and came and sat down. 'So you're defending that young barrister who sent Celia that horrid letter. Surely he must be a bit mad?'

'He's alleged to have sent the letter,' Rosa said. 'That doesn't necessarily mean he did send it.'

Mrs Spicer let out a small peel of laughter. 'How you lawyers love splitting hairs! I often used to say that to Celia.' She paused and her expression became clouded. 'It's terrible that the police haven't yet made an arrest. Surely they must know who did it?'

'It appears not.' Watching her hostess closely, Rosa went on, 'I can't help feeling it'll turn out to be somebody she knew quite well. Would that be your view too?'

Sidestepping the question, Mrs Spicer said, 'As you probably know, Celia, myself, old Mr Ackroyd and Giles Crowhurst used to meet for bridge at one of our homes every Thursday evening, but her death has brought all that to an end. I don't think Mr Ackroyd minds too much as he's been finding it an increasing effort to turn out at nights. He's over eighty, you know. But I miss our bridge evenings more than I can say, though I still play at my club. I tried to call Giles only this afternoon,' she went on, like a liner now steaming firmly ahead, 'but gathered he's in Brussels. He's got an important job with the EEC and will be moving there shortly. There's irony in the fact that Celia gave him the reference that got him the job. He told me that himself after her death. Of course, they'd known each other for years and I'm sure Giles would have liked to marry her, but she obviously had other views.' She paused and gazed reflectively into her glass. 'At times, she could be very offhand with him. I think he used to irritate her. Perhaps if he'd stood up for himself more she'd have given him greater respect. Don't get me wrong, dear! I'm sure she was very fond of him, but it didn't prevent her being cruel. It was a streak in her nature. I recall only one occasion when Giles did stick up for himself. We were playing at Celia's flat. It was the Thursday that person had shouted abuse at her in court . . .'

'I was there when it happened,' Rosa said.

'So you know all about it dear. Well, you would, anyway. As I was about to tell you, Norman, that's Mr Ackroyd, and I arrived together, but there was no sign of Giles. I thought he must be late, but Celia said rather testily that he'd arrived and was fetching himself a glass of water. When he appeared, she remarked in a very acid tone on the length of time it had taken him to get it. Instead of placating her the way he usually did, he answered her back with equal asperity. Said he'd also been washing his hands.' She stopped abruptly and gave Rosa a self-deprecating glance. 'Telling you about it now makes it sound terribly trivial, but somehow it's left an impression on my mind. I suppose because the worm unexpectedly turned. It also had its effect on the rest of the evening.'

'In what way?'

'Giles played very badly that evening, he didn't seem able to concentrate, and when we finished, he was the first to leave. Normally, when we played at Celia's flat, he'd stay behind and help her clear up. I said this to Celia after he'd gone and she merely remarked that he'd been in one of his moods. The truth is, however, I'd never seen him like that before. Clearly something had upset him that evening.' She put up a hand and gently patted her elegantly coiffured mound of golden hair. 'I only mention it, dear, because it showed Celia in one of her own unsympathetic moods.'

'I suppose that, over the years, she may have grown thoroughly bored with his attentions.'

'It was definitely more than that. I think there was another man in her life.'

'You mean Edward Maxwell?'

Mrs Spicer nodded. 'I've only learnt his name recently through the media. I've read that he's disappeared and the police are anxious to interview him.'

'Did Judge Kilby ever mention him?'

'Never by name. She would refer rather mysteriously to weekends in Sussex, but that was all. I gather Mr Maxwell lives near Horsham.'

'Yes. The significant thing about his disappearance is that he left home three days after Judge Kilby's death and though, I gather, she'd spent all the previous weekends at his home, she didn't go there the weekend she was killed.'

'Even though he was at home,' Adèle Spicer observed with a certain relish.

'Exactly.'

'So instead of *cherchez la femme*, it's *cherchez l'homme*,' she said with a roguish smile. 'Isn't that intriguing?'

'Would Giles Crowhurst be capable of murder?' Rosa asked suddenly.

Mrs Spicer looked at her aghast. 'Oh, no, he couldn't possibly have done it.'

'Not out of jealousy that another man had entered her life?'

Mrs Spicer shook her head vigorously. 'Giles had been suffering from unrequited love for so long it had become part of his existence. He could no more kill anyone than I could.'

Rosa refrained from comment, but reflected on the number of murders that were one-off crimes committed by hitherto exemplary citizens. People like Giles Crowhurst and Adèle Spicer. Everyone had a breaking point: a moment when he was within a hair's breadth of murder. Not all murderers had to be pathological paranoid schizophrenics straight from the psychiatrist's casebook.

'You've been most kind and helpful,' she said, getting up from her chair. 'I take it you don't know of anyone else who may have had a motive for murdering Judge Kilby?'

'*Cherchez l'homme*, dear,' Mrs Spicer said, clearly pleased with the phrase she had coined. 'In other words, find Mr Maxwell.'

Rosa took her leave and drove home in a reflective frame of mind. She was grateful to Robin for having suggested the visit. It wasn't that Adèle Spicer had come up with any startling revelations (that wasn't to be expected), but she had managed to set Rosa's thoughts flowing in a new direction.

CHAPTER 27

Jez had been told to get out of London and stay out until his employer signalled that it was safe for him to return.

He had gone to Bristol where Bernard Riscock had an old associate via whom communication could be made.

'Ever been to Bristol?' Riscock had asked. Jez had given his head a sullen shake. 'You'll like it there,' Riscock had added.

It had taken Jez less than half a day to know that he didn't like Bristol. He hadn't expected to and he didn't. He didn't like the beer and the first girl he tried to chat up laughed at his accent.

To Jez there was only one place to live and that was London; more specifically the area south of the river. He had been born and bred in Wandsworth, now lived in Merton and worked in Balham. He had been thinking of moving back to Wandsworth to live since his wife had walked out on him taking the two kids. The fact was he had been enjoying his new-found freedom when this had to happen. He had resented being packed off to Bristol and had decided after a couple of days that he wasn't going to stay there. He'd return to the smoke and lie low at his new girlfriend's place. Riscock didn't know of her existence so there was no danger from that quarter.

He'd only known Marcia two weeks before he'd had to get out of town. But she had a one-room flat in Clapham and he'd been made to feel at home there. Her live-in boyfriend had recently left and she was as much in need of company as he was.

The night he reached his decision to return to London he felt excited as a schoolboy on the last day of term. He reflected that the only times he hadn't minded being away from the capital were when he'd been on holiday on the Costa Brava in Spain. There he could lie on the beach surrounded by compatriots, drink English beer and eat fish and chips. The sun shone and though you were abroad it didn't feel like it with so many reminders of home all around.

The next morning he rose early and left the house before anyone was up. He'd paid a full week's rent in advance for his room – Riscock had, at least, despatched him with a generous supply of money – and so the woman who let out the rooms wouldn't have any cause for complaint. Nevertheless, he left her a note which read, 'Had to leave sudden.' To this he added a postscript, 'Gone up north,' just in case anybody came nosing around.

He caught an early train to London and felt an immediate upsurge of exhilaration as it sped through the western suburbs on its approach to Paddington Station. It had been a sore point that Riscock hadn't let him take his car to Bristol on the grounds that it could be too easily traced.

He walked confidently past a policeman who was standing by the ticket barrier and descended to the underground. At Waterloo he changed on to the Northern Line for a train to Clapham North. From there it was only a ten minute walk to where Marcia lived.

He wasn't sure whether he would find her at home at ten-thirty in the morning as she worked shift hours at a twenty-four hour café in the neighbourhood.

He ran up the steps to the house door and pressed the bell marked 'top floor'. He was about to give it a second jab when the door opened and a woman came out.

'Thanks,' he murmured as he pushed past her and dashed up the stairs, arriving breathless at the top.

He knocked on Marcia's door, but there was no response. It was a door with a single yale-type lock and had been forced almost as often as it had been more conventionally opened. Moreover, Jez was well acquainted with door-locks as a dentist with tooth decay.

He had just got the door open and observed that there was no Marcia in the room, when he turned and saw the woman he'd passed at the front door glaring at him through the bannister rails. At the top of the stairs stood a police constable eyeing him with justified suspicion. He had kept his helmet on as if to emphasise he wasn't paying a social call.

'I'm just visiting my girlfriend,' Jez said with a feeble grin.

The officer nodded. 'We'll go along to the station and sort things out there.'

'But this is Marcia's flat and she's my girlfriend. She's

expecting me,' he added desperately.

The officer was not to be deflected, however, and Jez was firmly escorted out of the house.

By the time Marcia arrived at the police station and claimed him as a friend, it was too late.

'And remember,' Riscock had said, 'If you do get picked up by the police, keep your mouth shut. Say nothing, except that you want a lawyer. It's your right, not some bloody favour on the part of a sharp-nosed officer. Got it?'

The trouble with that advice was it presupposed Jez having obeyed orders.

'If you do anything silly,' his employer had added in a menacing tone, 'I'll tie a stick of dynamite to your tail and personally light the fuse.'

'That's all right, Bernie,' he had replied. 'I know which side my bread is buttered on.'

The words now came uncomfortably back to him. He had been at the station for several hours and was feeling the strain.

'It's about time,' Chief Inspector Chantry said, 'you remembered which side your bread is buttered on.' Jez gave a nervous jump and Chantry went on, 'In other words you've got to decide between Riscock and us. Which of us can help you the most? It's as simple as that.'

'I know what I'd decide if I was in Jez's shoes, sir,' Sergeant Kirkbride put in. 'I've heard that Riscock can turn very nasty towards people who don't follow his instructions.'

Chantry gave Jez a long appraising stare. 'You're well and truly caught between the devil and the deep blue sea. But if you choose the latter, there's always a chance you could be thrown a lifebelt.'

'How do you mean?' Jez asked in a hoarse tone.

'Admit that it was Riscock who ordered you to cause the explosion at Aubusson Way and you'll be doing yourself a favour. But if you prefer to take the full blame yourself . . .'

'I was only doing what he told me to do,' Jez said in anguish. 'There'd been a genuine leak two days earlier and he thought we could use it to good effect.'

149

'By blowing up the house and everyone in it?'

'No, definitely not. We didn't want anyone to get hurt. The idea was to make it so that they'd have to get out. Then Bernie could cash in on the site.'

'Did Riscock have anything to do with Judge Kilby's death?' Chantry asked suddenly.

Jez shook his head. 'He didn't exactly go into mourning, but he never killed her.'

'How do you know?'

'I just do know. Anyway, he always got others to do his dirty work for him.'

'Like you?'

'Sometimes,' Jez said with a resigned shrug.

'Did he ever discuss killing her with you?'

'Never. And that's the truth.' He paused. 'If Bernie had arranged for her death, she'd have been shot. And there wouldn't have been any fancy notes pinned to the body.'

'Die the Riscock way.' Kirkbride murmured.

Though Chantry felt satisfied with the way the interview had gone, it was the satisfaction of a bronze medal winner who still had hopes of gaining a gold.

Jez had confessed his part and had implicated Riscock, though Riscock himself would undoubtedly prove to be a much tougher nut to crack. But the ultimate shape of the case could now be seen. Jez would plead guilty and receive a lighter sentence than otherwise in view of the help he had given the police. Thereafter the way would be open for him to give evidence against his employer.

All that would be something for the lawyers to sort out.

The fact remained that the letter threatening to murder and the explosion at Aubusson Way had become peripheral matters, as Detective Chief Superintendent Ingster, who now had overall charge of the enquiry, was fond of somewhat aggressively pointing out. Chantry had no complaints about the new man in charge, though that didn't prevent his praying that his own reputation might eventually be vindicated.

When he arrived back at murder headquarters from the station where he had been interviewing Jez, he was told that

150

Rosa had been trying to get in touch with him. He decided to return her call immediately.

He listened in silence as she related what had happened between her client and Tony Kilby.

'What do you want me to do about it?' he asked when she finished. 'If Duxbury wants to take out a summons for assault, that's up to him.'

'I think he's less interested in that than that you should re-examine the possiblity of Kilby having murdered his mother.'

'He has an alibi. After saying good night to his mother he went straight back to his hotel and became involved in a poker game with four other men. It went on till six in the morning and they all vouch that he was with them the whole time.'

'Could it be a concocted alibi? A bit of collusion on the part of his friends.'

'We checked that, of course. The answer is they weren't his friends. They were five young men, two Canadians, a New Zealander, a Dutchman and Kilby who came together for-tuitously that evening. Nothing remarkable about that in Earl's Court. The Canadians had booked into the hotel mid-week, the New Zealander and the Dutchman only that day. The party was in progress in the room next to Kilby's when he got back and he went to investigate the noise. The others recall his joining them around eleven, as they were running out of beer and there was a discussion about whether the off-licence would still be open.'

'Sounds like a watertight alibi,' Rosa remarked. 'May I pass the information on to my client?'

'If you want. You might also tell him he's not cut out for the role of private eye.'

'Meanwhile no further progress?' Rosa asked.

'We've still got various lines of enquiry to follow up,' Chantry said in a cagy tone.

'Such as Edward Maxwell's whereabouts?'

'We'd certainly like to eliminate him if we can.'

'Have you tried looking for him in Portugal?'

'Why do you ask that?' Chantry said suspiciously.

'He employs a Portuguese couple and I understand that he

speaks the language. I'm just putting two and two together.'

'And not making five either,' Chantry remarked and rang off after a brisk goodbye.

CHAPTER 28

Edward Maxwell left Lisbon just twenty-four hours before the local police, tipped off by Interpol, came looking for him.

He flew first to Madrid and then on to Frankfurt. From there he caught a plane to Brussels. He bought a separate ticket for each leg of his journey in order to lessen the chances of being traced.

His object was to slip back into England unannounced and unobserved.

With the various changes of plan it took him the best part of a day to complete his journey. On his arrival in Brussels he checked in at a large, impersonal hotel which would ensure him anonymity. It was not the hotel he normally stayed at in the city.

It was Thursday and he decided that Saturday would be the best day to complete his journey. It would be one of the busiest weekends for cross-channel travellers. With this in mind he went out and bought a single ticket to London via Ostende and Dover.

He returned to the hotel, satisfied with the arrangements he had made for his return. Provided they weren't thwarted, then nothing would happen until he was ready.

It was after his return to England that he decided to create a diversion. The police investigation was clearly in a doldrum and required a cathartic jolt. A false lead would give them something to energise their stagnating minds.

There wasn't any doubt that Peter Chen could cook Peking Duck as well as any chef in town. It was one of Rosa's favourite dishes and he had promised to cook it the next time she came to dinner at his flat. He had then promptly set the date for the next evening. This, he said, would give him time to buy a duck, scald it in boiling water and leave it hanging in the kitchen overnight.

Rosa accepted the invitation with alacrity, not merely to partake of Peking Duck, but because she wanted to try out a new theory on Peter concerning the murder. The only trouble with it was her inability to prove it.

Whenever he cooked dinner for her, she always arrived by taxi so as not to interrupt his culinary work by fetching her and, less importantly, so as to be free to drink without worrying about driving afterwards.

Delicious smells were coming through the front door before he opened it. There was a flurry of sound within and he appeared wearing a bright orange apron. He almost yanked Rosa through the door; then gave her a quick kiss and disappeared in the direction of the kitchen.

'I've just got to make the pancakes,' he called over his shoulder. 'Go help yourself to a drink.'

Rosa went into the living-room and poured herself a Punt e Mes. She'd never cared for the taste, but regarded it as the right drink to sip before a rich Chinese meal. She persuaded herself that it got the digestion ready for what was to come.

'Dinner will be served in thirty minutes,' he announced, coming into the room and flopping into a chair. 'I wouldn't go to all this trouble for anyone else. So what's happening? You said something on the phone about Duxbury being in a punch-up with Kilby's son.'

Rosa nodded and told him what had occurred.

'Getting involved with Duxbury is the worst thing that's ever happened to you,' he said with a prolonged sigh. 'Once upon a time he could have been shipped off to the colonies, but what's to be done with him now?'

'Everything will depend on how his case is resolved.'

'The fact that Judge Kilby was generally unpopular can only help him. I can't see a judge sending him to prison.'

Leaving Rosa sipping her drink and endeavouring not to make a face, he returned to the kitchen. Some minutes later he gave her a shout to join him.

The dining alcove was at one end of the kitchen, furnished in

153

bamboo. On the table a slender red candle cast a soft flickering light. Cutlery gleamed and there was an array of wine glasses beside each plate. Rosa gave a little exclamation of delight.

'I thought it was time to lay the table properly before I forgot how,' he said, pleased with her reaction.

He fetched a pan from the stove and served Rosa with jumbo prawns in a spicy sauce. The Peking Duck followed, succulent pieces of bird waiting to be wrapped in the pancakes with sliced cucumber and spring onions.

'Just to be original, I thought we'd finish with lichees out of a tin,' he said as he removed their plates.

'That was absolutely delicious,' Rosa said appreciatively. 'Now come and sit down and let me tell you what's occupying my mind.'

He listened with grave attention as she propounded her theory.

'But I don't see how I can ever prove it,' she said at the end. 'Or disprove it, for that matter. And it's not enough to pass on to the police as it stands.'

Peter looked thoughtful for a while. 'I may be able to help,' he said at length.

'How?'

He took hold of her hand and interleaved his fingers with hers. 'It's always a question of knowing someone in the right place,' he said with a boyish grin. 'Let's have coffee in the other room and I'll tell you.'

'What do you make of this?' Chief Superintendent Ingster asked, handing Chantry the letter he had been reading. 'Came in the morning's post.'

Chantry took it. On a single sheet of white paper, now encased in a cellophane envelope, was typed: '*Try checking Crowhurst's set of kitchen knives.*'

'Have we?' Ingster went on.

'No, sir. We haven't checked anyone's, except for Duxbury's at the cottage near Guildford. As you know, there were no fingerprints on the murder weapon and we've failed to trace it

154

to anyone.' He glanced again at the piece of paper in his hand. 'Where was this posted?'

'Wimbledon. Caught the last collection yesterday evening.' He pushed the envelope across his desk for Chantry to see.

It was also typed and addressed to: *Judge Kilby Murder Headquarters, London S.W.*

'The post office delivered it to the right place first time round,' Ingster added sardonically.

'What do you propose doing, sir?'

'What else is there to do other than pay Mr Crowhurst a visit and ask if we can count his knives?'

'If you ask me, sir, it's a hoax.'

'You may be right. On the other hand it may be a genuine lead. There's only one way to find out.'

CHAPTER 29

It seemed to Giles Crowhurst that the police had scarcely phoned before they were on his doorstep. He stopped what he was doing when the bell rang and went to let them in.

'Mr Crowhurst? I'm Detective Chief Superintendent Ingster. I believe you already know Chief Inspector Chantry.' He was a man of massive build and seemed to take up a disproportionate amount of space in Crowhurst's flat. He glanced around him with eyes that seldom missed anything. 'I see we've interrupted your packing.'

'I was making a start on my books. I hoped I'd be able to discard some, but when it comes to it, I find I can't. I shall have even less space when I move than I have here.'

'I heard you were leaving,' Ingster said, still looking about him. 'Joining that well-heeled band of untaxed servants in the Common Market, I gather. I'm afraid I was one of those who was dead against our becoming part of that outfit from the very start and certainly nothing's happened since to change my mind. And now we're threatened with the channel tunnel, as if we weren't close enough to Europe without that.' He turned

155

and fixed Crowhurst with an uncompromising stare. 'As you can tell, I'm a little Englander.'

'All six and a half feet of you?' Crowhurst murmured sardonically.

'Well, enough of all that, so let's get down to business. Business in this instance being this letter.' He gestured to Chantry to produce it from the briefcase he was carrying. The typed sheet of paper and the envelope were separately encased in cellophane and he put them down side by side on the table. 'Read that, Mr Crowhurst.'

Giles Crowhurst did as he was bidden with an increasing frown.

'I don't understand,' he said, looking up. 'Where'd this come from?'

'It arrived through the post this morning. That's all I can tell you at the moment. Somebody's obviously suggesting that the murder weapon came from here.'

'Somebody's got a very malicious sense of humour.'

'The point is, do you have a set of kitchen knives, Mr Crowhurst? And if so, may I see them?'

With a somewhat over-dramatic gesture, Crowhurst pointed at the tiny kitchen.

'Go and look for yourself,' he said. Ingster nodded to Chantry who stepped through the doorway to make a search.

'No set of knives here, sir,' he said after much opening of drawers and cupboards.

'Have you ever had a set of kitchen knives?' Ingster asked.

'As a matter of fact I have. I was given a set as a Christmas present a couple of years ago.' With a small twisted smile he added, 'Judge Kilby gave them to me.'

'What happened to them?'

'I gave them away. They were of no use to me.'

'I wonder why Judge Kilby gave you something you'd find useless?'

'I suspect she was passing on something that had been given to her. It wouldn't have been the first time she'd searched her bottom drawer for a present to give someone.'

'And you did the same thing?'

156

'Yes, I gave them to a cousin who was getting married.'

'Mind telling me the name of your cousin?'

'Rupert Bastin. He's an accountant in York and married a girl up there last summer. I didn't attend the wedding and I've never met his wife, but I can give you their address if you'd like to have it. If you do check on what I've told you, I'd be grateful if you'd do it tactfully. I don't want my cousin to think I'm involved in a murder enquiry.'

'Would he know about your friendship with Judge Kilby?'

'I very much doubt it. His mother and I are first cousins, but we hardly ever see one another. The invitation to Rupert's wedding was our only contact for years, if you don't count an annual exchange of Christmas cards.'

'I assure you we'll be as discreet as we can.' He turned his attention back to the anonymous letter lying on the table. 'Any idea who might want to make mischief for you?'

'Mischief is hardly the word I'd use,' Crowhurst said with feeling. 'It's a diabolical attempt to implicate me. As to who wrote it, I suggest you address your question to the man whose name, I believe, is Edward Maxwell. I've never met him, but it could well be in his interest to divert attention from himself.'

'How would he know you'd ever had a set of kitchen knives?' Ingster asked doubtfully.

'It doesn't stretch the imagination to believe that he was aware of my existence and knew a good deal more about me than I ever did about him.' Crowhurst's tone carried a note of bitterness.

Ingster nodded slowly. 'Well, thank you for your help, Mr Crowhurst. With luck we shan't need to trouble you again. We'll leave you to get on with your packing. I hope you'll enjoy life across the channel.'

'I'm sure I shall. Unlike yourself, I see the EEC as Europe's great hope.'

'Funny sort of bloke,' Ingster observed to Chantry as they went down in the lift. 'Bit like a lap dog, but with a poisonous fang.'

157

CHAPTER 30

Four men sat at a well-polished table in the Bloomsbury office of Gilbert Hickstead, the senior partner in a well-established firm of family solicitors. The other three were his client, Edward Maxwell, Chief Superintendent Ingster and Chief Inspector Chantry.

Hickstead had phoned the police the previous evening to say that his client had just returned to England and understood that the officers investigating Judge Kilby's death wished to interview him.

If they cared to come to Mr Hickstead's office at four o'clock the next afternoon, Mr Maxwell would be there and, subject to legal advice, would give them such assistance as he could.

When Ingster had said he would prefer the interview to take place at the police station, Mr Hickstead said, 'Very probably,' but that wouldn't suit him or his client.

In the circumstances, Ingster had had no option but to agree. The consequence was, however, that he arrived at the solicitor's office in an aggressive mood.

'If he gives me half an opportunity, I'll arrest him on the spot,' he had said to Chantry when they were on their way.

Gilbert Hickstead's firm rarely handled crime. Occasionally one of their clients would be charged with some peccadillo, but that was their sole involvement with the criminal law. To hold the hand of a client who was being interviewed by police in connection with a notorious murder was a new experience for the senior partner after forty years in the law. Not that he betrayed any sign of being daunted by the occasion.

He seated himself at one end of the table, as though about to chair a meeting. Maxwell sat on his right and the officers on his left.

'Well, gentlemen,' he said, when everyone was sitting down, 'shall we begin?'

Ingster produced a sheaf of notes and laid them on the table in front of him.

'Do you admit that you knew Judge Celia Kilby?' he asked.

'Certainly I knew her.'

'Used she to visit you at your home near Horsham?'

'Yes.'

'Spend weekends there with you?'

'Yes.'

'Were you lovers?' Ingster asked, leaning forward.

'Looking back on our relationship, I don't think there was ever much love in it on her part.'

'Were you in love with her?'

'I certainly wasn't infatuated. It was a companionable relationship. I think that describes it best.' He paused. 'While it lasted, that is. Which wasn't very long.'

'But it had its sexual side?' Ingster said, like a dog gnawing at a juicy bone.

'Yes.'

'Was that side more important to you than to her?'

Mr Hickstead flinched, but his client appeared unruffled by the question.

'I've no reason to think so,' Maxwell said after a slight hesitation.

'When did you first meet?'

'Last February.'

'Where?'

'At a reception at the Mansion House.'

'Did you become lovers straight away?'

'No. We went out to dinner after the reception – we'd each been there on our own – found we got on rather well and arranged to meet again.'

'Did you go to considerable lengths to keep your affair secret?'

'Yes,' Maxwell said simply, to Ingster's obvious surprise.

'Why?'

'Because it was in both our interests to behave with discretion. Particularly Celia's.'

'Is it correct that she spent the four weekends preceding her death at your home?'

'You've clearly checked, so I accept that you're right.'

'But you didn't have any arrangement to meet the weekend she was killed?'

'No.'

'Why not?'

Maxwell plucked at his lower lip before answering. It was the first time he had shown any sign of fidgeting and it didn't go unnoticed by the officers.

'We decided to give it a rest that weekend,' he said, refusing to meet Ingster's gaze.

'Had you had a row?'

'No.'

'But quite suddenly this pattern of weekend visits is broken. There must have been a reason.'

'You make it sound too dramatic. It wasn't like that.'

'It strikes me as a very remarkable coincidence that the first weekend Judge Kilby doesn't spend with you, she's murdered.'

'That's a comment you'll hardly expect my client to respond to,' Mr Hickstead said in a reproving tone.

Ignoring the intervention, Ingster went on, 'Well, it is a remarkable coincidence, isn't it, Mr Maxwell?'

'Life's full of coincidences,' Maxwell said with a shrug. 'I can only tell you the facts as I know them.'

'Would you care to tell me where you spent that Saturday evening?'

'At home, watching television as far as I remember. I probably also read a bit. It was no different from most of my evenings at home.'

'You didn't by any chance get your car out and drive up to Aubusson Way?'

'I did not.'

'It wouldn't have taken you long to get there and back. What would it be, about thirty-five miles each way?'

'If you say so. For your further information, I've never been to Celia Kilby's flat.'

'When did you first learn of her death?'

'On the radio on Sunday.'

'What did you do?'

'I didn't do anything. Our relationship had been entirely sub rosa. Moreover, I didn't know any of her friends, so there was nothing I could do.'

'Did it never occur to you to get in touch with the police?'

'Of course it occurred to me,' he said, shifting uncomfortably in his chair. 'But, as I've already explained, our relationship was known only to ourselves, which was the way we wanted to keep it. If I'd thought I could be of any help, I would have got in touch. As it was, my overriding thought was not to become involved.'

'A thoroughly reprehensible attitude for a responsible citizen, wouldn't you say?'

'With hindsight, I agree it might have been better if I had come forward at the time. Though I still don't know how I could have helped.'

'You certainly didn't help by vanishing a few days after the murder. Why did you do that?'

'I had business to attend to in Lisbon. As you probably know by now, I have a flat there.'

'Is it another coincidence that you chose to disappear at that particular moment?'

'I advise my client not to answer that improper question,' Mr Hickstead broke in.

'You can see how black things begin to look against you?' Ingster went on, again ignoring the solicitor.

'I never murdered Celia Kilby, if that's what you're suggesting.'

'So why did you behave as if you had?'

'Really!' Mr Hickstead exploded. 'If you can't conduct yourself properly, I shall advise my client to discontinue the interview.'

Ingster turned his head and glared.

'That wouldn't be good advice. Not good advice at all.' He swung back to face Maxwell. 'What decided you to return on Saturday?'

'I'd finished my business. I'd also had time to reflect on events and realised it would be best if I came back and made myself available for interview.'

'Is that why you crept into the country on a cross-channel ferry instead of flying direct?'

'I had a day's business in Brussels on my way back and thought I'd return by rail and boat, which was something I hadn't done for thirty years.'

161

'Just another of life's coincidences, I suppose,' Ingster remarked with a sneer.

Maxwell glowered and his solicitor looked portentously disapproving.'

'Does the name Giles Crowhurst mean anything to you?' Ingster now asked, fixing Maxwell with a hard stare.

For a second he appeared nonplussed. 'Crowhurst? Crowhurst? I seem to have heard the name somewhere ... Wait a moment, wasn't he a barrister friend of Celia Kilby's?'

'Right first time. Did she often refer to him?'

'No. I seem to recall she found him rather a pain in the neck. Why do you ask?'

Ingster extracted the anonymous letter from his sheaf of notes and slid it across the table.

'Are you the author of that?' he barked.

'Let me see it!' Mr Hickstead said anxiously, as Edward Maxwell reached for the cellophane envelope.

'I don't know what you're getting at,' Maxwell said in a strained tone. 'I certainly had nothing to do with this ... this document.'

Twenty minutes later, Ingster and Chantry drove away from the solicitor's office.

'If forensic can't help us nail some of those lies and half-truths we've just been fed, then nobody can,' Ingster said when they were in the car. 'We're going to the lab now to tell them just that.'

CHAPTER 31

Two days later Giles Crowhurst dined with Robert Tangley, the head of his Chambers, at the latter's club.

Tangley was in the bar when Crowhurst arrived and came across to greet him.

'Good to see you, Giles, what'll you have?'

'A gin and tonic, please.'

'And I'll have another bloody mary,' he said to the barman who was waiting to serve them. 'So you're off tomorrow. I expect you'll be glad to get settled after all the to-ing and fro-ing. We're going to miss you in Chambers, Giles,' he went on with grating affability, 'but I'm sure we'll still see you when you're back in the country.'

'That'll certainly be my hope, too.'

'I'm certain you've made the right decision. The Bar can keep a very seductive hold on its members, but it's best not to delay a change of course when that's called for. You've had the good sense to realise that. Not everybody has. Our profession has always tended to have too many hangers-on.' He raised his glass. 'Cheers and the very best of good fortune in your new job.'

'Thank you, Robert. I shall certainly miss the camaraderie of the Bar, but one can't afford to be too sentimental about these things.'

'Exactly.' Lowering his voice, Tangley went on, 'We all know you've been through a rough time these past few weeks and a complete change of scene is probably what you need more than anything else. The shadow of Celia's death hangs over all of us, but I realise you were especially fond of her and must have been deeply affected by what happened. I just wish to God the police could clear the whole matter up and make an arrest. I gather they've now found the fellow she used to visit at weekends and no doubt they're putting him through the mill.'

'You think he did it then?'

'He seems the most likely suspect. I never believed it was Duxbury or any of the other peripheral characters. None of them had sufficient motive.' He assumed a contemplative air. 'Remarkable woman, Celia. She really ought to have been a man. She had a man's mind, you know. Personally, I always regarded her as a bit of a dark horse.'

'I'm not sure I agree...'

'Oh, but she did, Giles. She never really came to terms with her womanhood.'

Crowhurst thought his head of Chambers was talking rubbish, but had no inclination to tell him so. Instead he finished his drink and accepted another.

Twenty minutes later when they went down to dinner,

Tangley was talking about himself and continued to do so throughout the meal. Crowhurst was content to enjoy the food and the wine and to make the right noises at the right intervals.

By eleven o'clock he was more than ready to go home.

'Well, *au revoir*, Giles,' Tangley said as they parted on the steps leading down to the pavement. 'Making an early start, are you?'

'Yes.'

'Flying, I suppose?'

'No, I'm taking my car. It seemed the easiest way of transporting a lot of my bits and pieces.'

'Yes, of course.'

'But I'll still have to come back to clear up various odds and ends I've not been able to deal with.'

'Don't forget to drop in and see us when you do.'

It was with a sigh of relief that Crowhurst found a taxi and went home. His car was already loaded and he intended setting out for Dover before the rush-hour traffic built up the next morning.

In the event he made such a good start that he was clear of London by eight o'clock. With so much time in hand, he decided to stop for breakfast on the way. He had only had a cup of coffee before leaving and was feeling distinctly peckish. He supposed that excitement had given an edge to his appetite.

As he ate, he recalled how he had enthused about the prospect of working in Brussels to Celia Kilby and had tried to excite her imagination with visions of their spending weekends together on both sides of the channel. She had quickly, however, put a dampener on that. It was about the same time as he learnt of Edward Maxwell's existence (though he wasn't aware of his name until later) and of the weekends she was spending at his home.

Despite all the rebuffs, he had gone on hoping that one day she would agree to marry him. He had been prepared to wait. Her ice-maiden image had held him in thrall since they first met in Chambers all those years ago.

'A bit of a dark horse,' Tangley had called her. In one sense, he supposed she was. This was borne out by the fact that not even he had been aware of the existence of an illegitimate son. But one thing she most certainly had never been and that was a stereotype.

In the weeks that had passed since her death, he had struggled to come to terms with life without her. His move to Brussels was a necessary part of his rehabilitation. Indeed, it had become his only option.

He arrived in Dover with time to spare and found himself first in line for embarkation. It was a fine, sunny day and the sea was sparklingly blue. He opened the car window and settled back to read the paper.

Later he left the car to present himself for passport and Customs inspection, both of which were painless procedures. A middle-aged barrister travelling alone didn't arouse suspicion. He resembled neither a soccer hooligan nor a drug smuggler.

He was on his way back to the car when he noticed a man peering intently through the driver's window into the interior.

He frowned, wondering what the person was up to. An elderly Ford Fiesta was not the sort of car to awake the interest of an *aficionado*.

He had almost reached the car when the man turned and straightened up.

'Good morning, Mr Crowhurst,' Chief Inspector Chantry said. 'I'd be glad if you'd accompany me to the police office over there. Don't worry about your car, we'll make sure it comes to no harm.'

'What's all this about?' Crowhurst said shakily, when he found his voice.

'I'm sure you don't really need to ask that, sir. But, as you have, Judge Kilby's murder is the answer.'

Giles Crowhurst's legs seemed to buckle, but Chantry saved him from falling, thereafter maintaining a firm grip on his arm until they were inside the building.

CHAPTER 32

It had been the previous afternoon when Rosa had phoned Chantry with her information. She wanted him to get any credit that was going for, despite everything that had happened, she regarded him as a fundamentally decent officer who had come off badly, even if it was partly his own fault.

'Yes, Miss Epton,' he had said somewhat wearily when they were connected, 'what now?'

His tone was very different when Rosa told him what she had found out.

'We'll have to make our own check through official channels, of course,' he said, 'but that sounds extremely interesting. How did you get on to it?'

'Through a friend who knows somebody over there,' Rosa said.

'But what made you suspect it in the first place?'

'I went and saw Mrs Spicer last week and we had a long talk. She mentioned one of their bridge evenings at Judge Kilby's flat when Crowhurst had behaved out of character. He had played badly that evening and appeared generally out of sorts. She said that when she arrived Crowhurst wasn't in the room and that Judge Kilby had remarked rather testily that he was fetching himself a glass of water. As soon as he came into the room it was apparent he wasn't his usual equable self.

'Later I was thinking back over what Mrs Spicer had said and recalled that when I'd been to see Giles Crowhurst he'd told me how he had learnt of Anthony Kilby's existence by seeing a letter from him on her desk which he had read, and how furious she had been when she caught him in the act. Anyway, it set me wondering whether he mightn't have been snooping again when he was supposedly fetching his glass of water. If so, what could he have seen that caused his demeanour to change so abruptly?

'He'd told me how she had written him a reference for the job in Brussels. Knowing how she regarded him, I assumed she had swallowed her principles and given him a glowing testimonial in order to get him out of her hair. On the other hand she didn't seem the sort of person who ever swallowed her principles.

'I then wondered if he might have seen a copy of the reference she wrote for him and supposing it wasn't all it should have been . . .

'The friend I mentioned has a senior contact over in Brussels who was able to make the necessary check. The answer was that her reference had killed any chance Crowhurst ever had of getting the post. Judge Kilby didn't even bother to damn him with faint praise and he was never called for interview. It was a stab in the back he was clearly determined to avenge.'

'What's happened to the carbon copy of the reference, I wonder?'

'I imagine that, after he'd killed her, he took her keys from her handbag, went up to her flat and retrieved it. At the same time he wrote the note which he subsequently pinned to the body.'

'I can see now why he's had to pretend to everyone that he'd got the job and was moving to Brussels.'

'He didn't have any other option if people weren't to start asking awkward questions.'

There was a silence. Then Chantry said in a tone of quiet sincerity, 'Thanks, Miss Epton.'

It was approximately twenty-four hours later when they spoke again.

'I'm in Dover, Miss Epton. Your theorising was spot on. We detained him just as he was about to board the Ostende ferry.'

'Has he talked?'

'He's told us everything. Almost as if it was a relief to get it off his chest.'

'It probably was. I don't find that hard to understand.'

'Maybe not.'

'After all, he's not a hardened criminal,' Rosa went on. 'Just a man who was driven over the edge and has had to live with his conscience ever since.'

Chantry was silent for a moment. 'I haven't told you about the anonymous letter we received a few days ago,' he said, and proceeded to relate what had happened. 'Crowhurst decided to send it when he got back from a visit to Brussels last week. It

167

was a crude attempt to attract suspicion which he knew he'd have no difficulty in refuting. When we interviewed him about it, he suggested that Edward Maxwell must have been its author.' He paused. 'His conscience was plainly not troubling him too much that day.'

'The human conscience is an unpredictable piece of mechanism,' Rosa remarked. 'It doesn't always react when it should, but that doesn't mean it's out of order.'

'I'm only a simple policeman, Miss Epton, but thanks again.'

CHAPTER 33

In the weeks and months that followed a number of trials took place.

The first, in order of time, was Giles Crowhurst's. From the moment of his arrest at Dover he had never wavered in his determination to plead guilty. It seemed that everyone, including himself, wanted this particular chapter closed as quickly as possible. It had too many uncomfortable reminders to be left unfinished for longer than necessary.

In view of his attitude the prosecution was able to cut a few corners and the trial itself lasted but a matter of minutes. As the only penalty for murder was the statutory one of imprisonment for life, there was nothing for defending counsel to say in mitigation of sentence and the judge sensibly refrained from sermonising on the wickedness of what he had done. Indeed, he gave the impression of being as anxious as anyone to get the defendant in and out of his court with the minimum of delay. He clearly viewed the case with the utmost distaste.

Some weeks later, Bernard Riscock and Jez appeared in the same court but before a different judge. Jez pleaded guilty to causing an explosion and then turned Queen's evidence to testify for the prosecution against his employer. A blood-letting contest ensued and after a three-day trial, the jury found Riscock guilty of the same offence, in his case of having planned and directed the crime. Jez received a sentence of three years' imprisonment and his employer one of double that.

It was a further two months before Peter Duxbury appeared in the dock and pleaded guilty to a charge of sending a letter threatening to murder.

Rosa had briefed one of the Bar's most silver-tongued advocates to defend. They had discussed the case from every angle and, in particular, had considered whether it might be successfully argued that the wording of the letter didn't actually amount to a threat to murder. But, as counsel pointed out, if that defence failed, it would make any plea in mitigation infinitely harder and the judge, who was newly appointed and an unknown quantity, might pass a custodial sentence. They therefore agreed that it would be better to plead guilty and mitigate like mad, stressing the provocation he had received, the agony of suspense he had undergone and the fact that he had decided to quit the Bar and go and work for his uncle who farmed in Ireland. For Rosa, this course also obviated any question of her being placed in a moral dilemma by virtue of Duxbury's initial admission to her.

As she sat in court admiring the artistry with which the plea in mitigation was being woven, her mind went back to the first time she met Peter Duxbury. The disastrous occasion when he turned up in Judge Kilby's court to make a similar plea on behalf of Cedric Duthie, the stealer of ladies' underwear. Except that the comparison was more between a smooth and expensive claret and a bottle of red plonk. Also in sharp contrast were the politely attentive demeanour of today's judge and the brutal counsel-baiting of Judge Kilby.

Eventually, defending counsel sat down and the defendant was asked if he had anything to say before sentence was passed.

Rosa held her breath for a moment, but was relieved when Peter Duxbury merely gave a numb shake of his head.

'Peter Irving Duxbury,' the judge said fixing him with a cool, appraising look, 'the less I say about this reprehensible matter, the better. I accept everything your counsel has so eloquently said on your behalf and have decided that the appropriate penalty will be a fine of two hundred and fifty pounds.'

It was at home that evening that the judge's wife enquired about the case and he told her the result.

'I shall never forget the day you came home after appearing before Judge Kilby,' she said. 'It was your first case as a QC.'

He nodded. 'She was certainly determined to show no favours to a so-called up and coming silk.'

'And now you're a High Court judge,' she said proudly.

'At least I had the sense not to commit my sentiments to paper,' he remarked with a faint smile.

That same evening, Rosa had a phone call from Peter Chen.

'I've got to go over to Paris this weekend,' he said. 'Will you come?'

'Yes,' she replied without hesitation.